Billy's Blitz

Billy's Blitz

Barbara Mitchelhill

ANDERSEN PRESS • LONDON

First published in 2014 by
Andersen Press Limited
20 Vauxhall Bridge Road
London SW1V 2SA
www.andersenpress.co.uk

2 4 6 8 10 9 7 5 3 1

British Library Cataloguing in Publication Data available.

ISBN 978 1 78344 085 6

Printed and bound in Great Britain by CPI Group (UK) Ltd,
Croydon CR0 4YY

For Noon, Harley, Sally and Chris

One

Birthday surprise

Have you ever had one of those nights when you can't sleep?
And you lie in bed tossing and turning? That was me, the night
before my twelfth birthday. I lay there in the dark, eyes wide
open, even though I couldn't see a thing.

Mum had put up blackout curtains, and I didn't like 'em
one bit.

'No use complaining, Billy,' she'd said. 'There's a war on. If
that Hitler sends his planes over Balham, they won't see any
lights from this house, that's for sure – or my name's not Ruby
Wilson!'

After that, my bedroom was black as a coal mine. There
wasn't so much as a pinhole of light got through those
curtains. Not that I was scared of the dark. Not me. Balham
boys ain't scared of nothing.

That night, when I couldn't sleep, I lay there thinking about
everything that had happened since my last birthday – good
and not so good.

The day I was eleven, I remember waking up to the smell
of bacon frying and leaping out of bed and rushing downstairs.

Bacon, egg and fried bread, that's what I had. It was a special treat for my birthday. Things weren't rationed then. Oh boy! They tasted good! And when I'd wiped the last trace of egg yolk with my bread, Dad said, 'I've got a present for you, Billy boy!'

I'd tried to guess what it was.

'Is it a football? A stamp album? New boots?'

Dad laughed and shook his head.

My little sister, Rose, who was five then, got excited. 'What is it, Dad?' she squealed, tugging at his sleeve and jumping up and down like a jack-in-a-box.

'Calm down, pickle,' Dad said and he lifted her up, giggling and wriggling, and beckoned me to follow him to the back door. Mum came with us – she must have been in on the secret cos Dad always told her everything.

We stepped out into the garden, which was long and thin and planted with vegetables: cabbages, carrots, turnips and potatoes. We used to have a lawn where I played football, but Dad had told us there was going to be a war with Germany and we'd need to grow our own food.

That day, Dad pointed to the far end of the garden. 'Go and look in the shed, Billy,' he said. 'See if you can find something in there.'

I raced over and flung the shed door open. It was quite dark inside and I couldn't see much till my eyes adjusted to the gloom. Then I saw it! Sitting on an old grey blanket was the most beautiful dog I'd ever seen. It was a young German shepherd with the loveliest, kindest eyes and a coat like black

2

velvet. I could hardly breathe, I was so excited. I'd always wanted a dog, see.

'She's yours, Billy,' said Mum with a big smile on her face. 'And she's wanting a good home.'

I reached out to stroke her and she jumped up, full of energy, wagging her tail non-stop and licking my hand as if she knew she was my dog.

Mum and Dad were standing by the door, watching. 'Is she really mine? Honest?' I asked, hardly believing it was true.

'She is,' Dad said, grinning from ear to ear. 'All she needs is a name.'

I looked into the dog's brown eyes and she gazed back at me as if she had known me all her life. That was when I knew she was special. And a special dog should have a special name. I thought for a minute. 'I think I'll call her Sheeba.'

'Good name,' said Dad coming over to stroke her soft back. He liked dogs. He'd been brought up on a farm, see. He was as pleased as I was to have Sheeba in the family. 'She's nine months old, son, and I know you'll take good care of her.'

'Course I will, Dad,' I said, wrapping my arms round her and nuzzling my face in her fur. I couldn't have been happier. It was my eleventh birthday and I had a dog!

Later, Dad said, 'It's a pity not everybody feels like that about dogs,' and he told me a terrible thing. Because we were expecting to go to war with Germany, people didn't want anything German in their houses – not German music, not even dogs with German names, such as dachshunds and German shepherds. 'So they get rid of 'em,' said Dad. 'Kick 'em out.'

'They ought to be ashamed of themselves, if you ask me,' said Mum. 'It's cruel. As if this beautiful dog has anything to do with the Nazis, eh?'

That afternoon, we all went out to give Sheeba her first walk as part of our family. I felt really proud when I walked down the road with her on the lead – especially when I saw my mates, Ken and Barry, and they came over to pat her. Once we reached Tooting Bec Common I let her off the lead and threw a ball. You should have seen her run! She went like the wind to catch it. She was brilliant! Rose had fun, too. She found sticks for Sheeba to carry but she kept calling her Sherbert, which made us laugh.

Right from the start, we all loved Sheeba, and my eleventh birthday was the best ever: the best present and the best cake with candles and my family singing 'Happy Birthday' round the table. My life was good. I was happy. But it didn't last.

Not long after my birthday, Britain declared war on Germany and Dad went and joined the army. We didn't want him to, but he said he had to go and do his bit.

'I can't have that Mr Hitler coming over here,' he told us. 'So I can't leave all the fighting to the other chaps, can I?'

When he signed up, they gave him a uniform. It was a funny khaki colour, but he looked ever so smart in it and he polished his boots till you could see your face in 'em. He even had his photo taken.

'This is so you won't forget your poor old dad,' he said when he brought it home.

He gave Rose a big hug. Mum got a sloppy kiss and he

winked at me. He was a joker, my dad. He always tried to put on a brave face and make us laugh even when he was going off to another country where the Nazis might be shooting at him. He didn't want us to feel sad, see.

'I'll be back home before you know it,' he said. 'I don't suppose this war's going to last long. We'll show them Germans, eh?'

After Dad left, Mum went into the kitchen and cried by the sink, holding her apron over her face. I'd never seen her cry before and she didn't know I'd seen her that time. But I had. I knew she was worrying about him already. Wondering if he'd come back home.

We put Dad's photo in a nice frame on the mantelpiece and every night we said, 'Good night, Dad,' to it before we went to bed. Mum always gave it a kiss and said, 'Sleep tight, Norman. Keep safe.'

Poor little Rose couldn't understand why Dad had gone and she sobbed herself to sleep for a long time. We tried to stay cheerful and wrote him letters and Rose drew him pictures of Sheeba, but we didn't hear a lot back. I expect Dad was busy looking for Nazis.

By the end of September there were already anti-aircraft guns on Clapham Common and lots of barrage balloons fixed with long cables and floating in the air. Rose liked them. She said they looked like silver elephants.

'They're doing a good job,' Mum told us. 'If ever them Jerry planes come flying over Balham, they'll get tangled up in them cables. That'll fix 'em, won't it?'

Balham's only a few miles from central London and Mum thought Hitler might one day try to bomb important buildings, like the Tower of London or Buckingham Palace. So far he hadn't tried anything like that, but she said it was best to be prepared. That's why they put up the barrage balloons.

When I went back to school after the summer holidays the headmaster told us we were going to be evacuated. The whole school! We were being sent to somewhere in the country so we'd be safe and out of the reach of the Nazis. We'd go on a train, he said, and stay with some kind people who would look after us. My school was going to Hertford and all the teachers would be with us too. My best mates Ken and Barry were really excited.

'It'll be like an adventure,' said Ken. 'We'll stick together – just the three of us – and we'll have a great time. It's in the country and I bet there'll be loads of trees to climb.'

'There might be a river we can swim in. That would be brilliant!' said Barry who was very keen on swimming and spent most of the summer – and winter – at the swimming baths in Elmfield Road.

But when Mum heard about the evacuation she wasn't so pleased.

'What an idea!' she said. 'No stranger's going to have my children. You're staying here so I can look after you properly,' she insisted. 'What are they thinking of? That Hitler's in Poland and that's a long way off. What's wrong with you staying here?'

So when the others went, I waved them off – and I was left behind, with no school and no friends.

As it turned out, Mum was right. The war seemed far away with the Nazis fighting in places I'd never heard of. Everything stayed the same in Balham except we'd all been given gas masks and petrol was rationed. Sometimes the anti-aircraft guns fired on Tooting Bec Common and the air-raid sirens sounded – but we knew it wasn't real. They were only practising. People were calling it the Phoney War.

Then Dad came home on a week's leave in December, two weeks before Christmas, and I helped him build an Anderson shelter in the back garden.

'Just in case Jerry starts dropping bombs,' Dad said. 'Then I'll know you'll be safe.'

The shelter was great! It had a curved tin roof, which Dad covered with the last bit of grass in the garden so a Nazi pilot looking down from his plane would hardly notice it. It was brilliant camouflage! Rose called it her little house and played inside, putting her teddy in the bunk beds.

I liked being with Dad and helping to build the shelter, but his leave was soon over. Just before he went back to the army, he gave Mum present. 'Here, Ruby darlin',' he said, handing her a little box. 'It'll be your birthday next week and I shan't be here – so it's an early surprise.'

Mum's eyes filled with tears as she opened the box. She ooohed and aaahhed and her cheeks flushed pink when she saw a pair of gold earrings like little hoops. 'Oh, Norman!' she squealed. 'They're gorgeous! Where did you find them?'

Dad just grinned and gave Mum a great big kiss. Then he hugged Rose and me before he set off down the road, waving goodbye, looking smart in his uniform. We were proud of him, but as soon as he'd gone I started to worry and I'm sure Mum did, too. We knew he was heading for danger and there was nothing we could do to keep him safe.

Soon after that, it was Christmas, but it felt empty without Dad. We sent him some biscuits and Mum knitted him a pair of socks, but we wished he could be home with us. Christmas didn't feel the same.

Then heavy snow came in January, and I helped Rose build a snowman in the garden. The snow stayed for ages and, before it finally disappeared, I heard that some of the kids who had been evacuated had been brought home by their parents.

'You see!' said Mum. 'I was right, wasn't I, Billy? Nothing's happened. We're safe as houses here. It was all a big fuss over nothing, if you ask me.'

But my mates Ken and Barry didn't come back. They stayed in Hertford – which was bad cos I didn't have nobody to play footie with or swap cigarette cards with. I missed them a lot. But, looking on the bright side, none of the teachers came back either, so our school couldn't open again and that meant I'd got plenty of time to do what I wanted.

Until Mum got a job.

'I'm going to work in Mr Lodey's garage,' she suddenly announced one day.

I was shocked! Mum had never had a job, see. She'd always stayed at home and looked after us like all the other mums.

Who was going to do the cooking? That's what I wanted to know.

'We'll manage, Billy,' she said. 'Mr Lodey needs help now his son's been called up.'

This sounded crazy to me. 'You won't be mending cars, will you?' I asked. She didn't know anything about engines. Dad knew loads.

Mum shook her head. 'Nothing like that, Billy. I'll be working on the petrol pumps. It's an important job now that petrol's rationed. Not a word to Dad though,' she said, tapping her nose. 'He thinks a woman's place is in the home and he'll only worry. But I say that while he's away fighting, I've got to help out and do my bit. It's only right.'

'What about me and Rose? What'll happen to us?'

She put her arm round my shoulder. 'Mrs Scott next door will look after both of you and you can help her with the shopping. It's hard for her with two babies and her husband away.'

Mrs Scott had twins called Lily and Grace. They were born at Christmas and they made a terrible racket. Always crying, they were. I could hear them through the wall at night.

'Do I *have* to do her shopping?' I groaned. Shopping was horrible. I'd done plenty for Mum. Shopping meant queuing for hours and by the time you reached the counter they'd often sold out of whatever you were queuing for. 'Do I *have* to, Mum?'

She raised an eyebrow and gave me one of her looks and I knew I couldn't wriggle out of it.

Mum started work at the garage in April that year. I did my best to help out – digging the veg patch, cleaning the house and sometimes pushing Mrs Scott's babies out in their pram. I showed Rose how to play marbles and how to kick a football. She wasn't bad for a girl. I even taught her reading and writing. I must say, she was a fast learner so when she sent a drawing to Dad, she could write her name underneath and later a whole sentence. I bet Dad liked that.

All this time the war was going on in Europe and I knew what was happening cos people talked about it all the time. Some of them had wireless sets, see. And then there was the news at the cinema. Mum took me to see *Gone with the Wind*, which was a brilliant new film in full Technicolor – I'd only ever seen black-and-white ones till then. Before the film started, the news came on and showed a place on the French coast called Dunkirk. Our soldiers were on the beaches trying to escape from the Germans. They were trapped there until loads of boats came across the Channel from England to rescue them. Some boats were really small – just little fishing boats – and it must have been dangerous travelling all that way. But somehow they managed to rescue hundreds of soldiers and take them back home. I thought they were really brave and I wished I could have been there to help out.

That summer was long and sunny and I often took Rose and Sheeba down to Tooting Bec Common. Rose liked looking at the barrage balloons and she gave them names like Silver Whale and Heffalump. Meanwhile I threw sticks for Sheeba. She loved chasing after them and brought them back to me, her tail wagging with pleasure, ready to go again.

There weren't many other dogs around because lots of people had theirs put down when the war started. They were worried that pets would eat too much and it would be difficult when food was rationed. I think that's disgusting. I'd rather starve than have Sheeba put down. We shared our food with her – that's what we did in our family.

Over those summer weeks I spent a lot of time training her. I taught her to sit and stay and when I held up my finger, or said no, I could stop her barking.

'She's ever so clever, ain't she, Billy?' said Rose, and I had to agree. She was a very intelligent dog.

When July came, the Nazis landed on the Channel Islands and Hitler tried to cross the Channel and invade England. But he hadn't reckoned on our pilots and their brilliant aircraft. They kept him out all right! A man told me there'd been air battles near Biggin Hill and they called it the Battle of Britain. Planes were shooting each other down, spinning out of control and plummeting to the ground. It must have been terrifying, but I wished I'd seen it. I wished I'd been there. Instead, I was shopping for Mrs Scott – the most boring thing in the world.

All those things had happened since my eleventh birthday. Now here I was – the night before my twelfth birthday, lying in bed, with Sheeba curled up on the rug. I didn't feel excited. There was nothing to get excited about. There was no Dad, no mates and probably no presents now that things were so difficult, what with the war and everything.

My thoughts were fizzing round in my head, but I finally closed my eyes and managed to drift off. I hadn't been sleeping long when I was woken by a noise downstairs. Sheeba growled softly under her breath and I said, 'No, Sheeba,' to quieten her while I listened again.

Rat-tat-tat. Someone was knocking at the front door.

It's never good news when somebody comes in the middle of the night. I sat up, wondering who it could be. I knew Mum hadn't heard the knocking cos I could hear her snoring in the next room.

Rat-tat-tat-tat-tat. The knocking came again.

'Mum!' I yelled and thumped on the wall. 'There's somebody at the door.'

The snoring stopped, but still she didn't answer. Sometimes she's slow to wake up.

Without waiting for her, I slid out of bed and hurried down the stairs towards the front door, the lino in the hall cold under my feet.

Rat-tat-tat.

'All right I'm coming!' I shouted.

A man's voice replied. 'About time, son!'

I gasped. I couldn't believe it. Dad was home!

I threw the bolts back, turned the key in the lock and flung the door open wide. Dad stepped inside and grabbed hold of me, swinging me off my feet while I clung to him, unable to speak, drawing in his smoky smell and thinking that this was the best birthday present I could have wished for.

Two

Just what I wanted

Suddenly, there was a shriek from Mum upstairs. 'NORMAN!' she screamed from the landing before flying down the stairs in her pink nightie, her curlers bouncing on her head. She was hysterical, and flung her arms round Dad, sobbing and squealing all at the same time.

After that, Rose rushed down shouting, 'Dad!' at the top of her voice and soon they were both squashing the breath out of him.

'Surprise, eh?' he said when they released him. 'Here I am turning up like a bad penny.' He grinned and dumped his kitbag on the floor. 'Pop the kettle on, will you, Ruby love? I ain't had a drink since this morning and I'm parched.'

Mum laughed. 'Course I will.' And we all went down to the kitchen and sat round the table while Mum put the kettle on the gas stove and two spoonsful of tea in the teapot.

Dad was wearing his uniform and looked pale and much thinner than when we'd last seen him. He seemed really tired, too, and kept rubbing at his face. Mum must have noticed cos she made him a couple of slices of toast and spread 'em with some jam she'd been saving.

'Thanks, Ruby,' he said as Mum gave him the cup of tea and he raised it to his lips. 'Ah! That tastes good that does. I ain't had a cuppa like this for months.'

Rose climbed up onto Dad's knee. 'Is the war over?' she asked. 'Are you staying here for ever now?'

'Just forty-eight hours, darlin',' he said, tickling her under her arm. 'But we're going to have fun, eh? We'll make it the best forty-eight hours ever.'

Mum's happy face vanished for a second. I think she was hoping he'd be staying longer. It was hard for her, not having Dad around, wondering where he was and if he was safe.

Dad noticed. 'Don't fret, Ruby love,' he said and squeezed her hand. 'We'll have a good time and I'll be back for longer next time.' Then he turned to me and slapped a hand on my shoulder. 'If I'm not mistaken it's your birthday tomorrow, ain't it, Billy boy? Couldn't miss that, could I?'

I grinned, glad that he'd remembered. Glad he was home so it would be a proper birthday.

'Twelve, eh?' he said.

I nodded.

'I'm six now,' said Rose and Dad kissed her on the forehead. 'So you are, Rosie girl,' he said. 'You'll be catching your brother up soon.'

He'd missed her birthday, and I could tell he felt bad about that. But he'd sent her a doll – a funny thing made out of cloth, with a lop-sided smile and yellow wool for hair. She called it Goldilocks and carried it everywhere.

14

He turned to me again.

'Well, Billy boy, I'll have to see if I can get you a present.' He grinned and winked at me. 'What do twelve-year-old boys like?'

Before I could answer, Mum said, 'It'll depend what you can get, Norman. Don't get his hopes up. It's not easy, with the war and everything. We don't have as much choice as we used to.'

But Dad wouldn't let that get in his way. 'Then I'll just have to work extra hard to find something, won't I? I got you them earrings, didn't I, Ruby?'

Mum blushed and touched the gold hoops she'd worn every day since her last birthday. I don't think she ever took them off. She loved them earrings.

'You're a clever one, Norman Wilson,' she said with a smile. 'I don't know how you do it.'

Dad winked again. 'Then I'll find something special for Billy,' he said. 'Don't you worry.'

When Dad had finished his tea and toast, we all went to bed. I was bursting with happiness that night. My dad was home, the next day was my birthday, and I couldn't help wondering what birthday present Dad could possibly find tomorrow.

The next morning Dad didn't get up when we did.

'Don't you kids go waking him,' said Mum. 'He needs his rest. It's hard work fighting them Nazis.'

When he did come downstairs, he was wearing a shirt and grey flannel trousers instead of his uniform. He looked really tired. There were circles under his eyes that were so dark I thought it would take him a week of sleeping to get rid of them. But he was glad to be home. I could tell that.

He sat down at the table and pulled Rose onto his knee.

'Where's that brother of yours, Rose?' he said, pretending he couldn't see me. Yet there I was standing only a few feet away.

Rose, who thought it was a good game, giggled and pointed at me. 'He's there, Dad! Have you forgotten it's his birthday?'

'Me? Forget Billy's birthday? I should think not! Come on, it's time we sang "Happy Birthday". Where's my banjo?'

His banjo was special. Silver and black it was. Beautiful! Dad could play loads of tunes and we'd sometimes sit around the fire and sing along. I loved that.

'I'll get your banjo, Dad,' I said and went to fetch it from the front room.

I handed it to Dad and stood waiting – blushing and feeling a bit embarrassed – but when he struck the strings of the banjo and the three of them sang 'Happy Birthday' I couldn't help grinning. Rose's voice was chirpy and quiet, Dad's was loud and very deep and Mum's was wobbly and high. As I listened, I felt very lucky to have my family with me, but I couldn't help wondering where we'd be on my next birthday and if we'd be together. I hoped so.

That morning, we celebrated Dad's homecoming and my birthday by having a fantastic breakfast of fried eggs. We didn't often have eggs since rationing, but Mrs Scott next door kept chickens in her back garden and she'd given Mum some especially for the occasion. They tasted delicious.

After we'd finished, Dad leaned back in his chair. 'Well, Ruby, my love,' he said, 'I don't get anything as tasty as that in the army.'

Mum smiled and gave him a cuddle and a kiss on his cheek.

Later, when he'd had a second cup of tea, he got up from his chair. 'I'd better be off if I'm going to find that present for Billy,' he said, ruffling my hair.

'I'll come with you, if you like,' I said.

'What? And spoil the surprise? No, you stay here, son, and I'll be back in the shake of a lamb's tail.' Then he walked down the hall, whistling like he always did, and out of the front door.

When he'd gone, Mum beckoned me over. 'I want you to go round to the garage, Billy,' she said in a whisper – though I don't know why, seeing that Dad had gone and wouldn't hear her. 'Tell Mr Lodey I won't be in today or tomorrow. Tell him your dad's home on leave.'

'Righto, Mum,' I said. 'I'll be as quick as I can.'

'But not a word to your dad!' she added.

The garage was up Bedford Hill not far from Tooting Bec Common. Mr Lodey was a nice old man who'd lived in Balham all his life. His son, Donald had joined the navy – I expect he missed him just like we missed Dad.

When I arrived at the garage, I walked into the wooden building behind the petrol pumps where Mr Lodey did repairs. He was lying flat on his back under an old lorry.

I bent down and called out, 'Hello, Mr Lodey.'

He slid out from under the lorry. 'Hello, Billy,' he said standing up and reaching for a rag to dry his hand. 'My goodness you're growing. You'll soon be as big as my Donald.' As he said it, his eyes glazed over and I guessed he was thinking about his son. 'He only had his nineteenth birthday two months ago,' he sighed. 'But they called him up to fight for his country so he had to go.'

I nodded. 'I expect he's very brave, Mr Lodey.'

The old man smiled. 'I expect so, Billy. Now, what can I do for you?'

'I've to tell you that Mum can't come in today or tomorrow,' I said. 'Dad's home on a forty-eight-hour pass. She says that she hopes you can manage.'

'You tell her not to worry. I can manage without her for a couple of days. Enjoy your time with your dad. I expect you miss him like I miss my Donald.'

When I got home, Mum was in the kitchen making a birthday cake. That was a surprise. We almost never had cakes. The day was getting better and better.

'Look, Billy!' Rose said, holding out her sticky hands. 'I helped make your cake. You can scrape the bowl, if you want.' She picked up the basin with the remains of the mixture in it and ran her finger round the edge. 'Mmm! It's good. You taste it.'

Somehow, she'd got a blob on the end of her nose and I couldn't help laughing.

The cake was in the oven and was almost cooked when Mum asked me to go and dig up some potatoes and carrots. 'I want to give your dad plenty to eat. He needs feeding up before he goes back.'

Sheeba came with me to fetch a fork from the shed. The ground was quite soft after the rain in the night so it was easy to dig. I'd almost filled a bucket with the veg when I heard Dad arrive home and shout, 'I'm back!' I threw the fork down and ran into the house with Sheeba racing after me, barking with excitement.

Dad was already in the kitchen, standing there with a grin as wide as a shovel.

'Did you manage to get anything, Dad?' I asked and held my breath waiting for the answer.

'Well, let me see,' he said very slowly, which drove me mad. He was just making me wait.

'Dad! Did you get me a present? Did you?'

'There just might be something for you.'

I grinned. 'Go on! Tell me! Where is it?'

'Well, if you take a look in the hall you might find something.'

I pushed past the table and burst through the door dying to see what he'd brought. But the hall was dark and at first I couldn't see anything that looked like a present. Not a parcel. Not a box. Not even an envelope. But then I saw a strange shape near the front door. A heap covered by a coat.

I ran and dragged the coat off. Underneath, there it was! A bike. A real, full-sized, grown-up bike with brakes and a lamp and everything!

Three

Dunkirk

'Wow! Where did you get it?' I asked, flinging my leg over the cross bar of my new bike to try it out. 'It's smashing, Dad!'

'I knew you needed a bigger one,' he said, walking down the hall. 'So I went to see Herbert's wife. You remember Herbert Chitterlow, my mate? We signed up for the army together.'

I nodded. I remembered Herbert.

'His wife said he wouldn't be needing his bike any more and she'd be glad for you to have it.' Dad went quiet as if there was something he wasn't telling me. I think Herbert must have been badly injured in the war. But I didn't like to ask.

When he didn't explain, I said, 'It's just what I wanted. Thanks, Dad.'

He nodded and smiled. 'It's a good bike, son. You look after it.'

Mum put my birthday cake on the table. 'Let's have a slice before we go out, eh?' she said, and cut a piece for each of us. It was delicious, a lovely sugary taste, which I hadn't had for ages.

Dad said we should go to the common. 'You ride your bike, Billy. We'll walk behind with Sheeba.'

I couldn't wait.

Mum made her hair look extra nice, all curly and gold. She put on her best frock and her Sunday hat. The two of them looked as proud as Punch as they walked down our road arm in arm with Dad whistling 'Doing the Lambeth Walk'. Rose was holding Dad's hand and Mum held Sheeba's lead while I rode in front on my brilliant full-sized bike. I couldn't believe how good it felt. My old one was too small and had fallen apart a long time since. This one was just the job for a twelve-year-old boy with long, skinny legs.

It was a great afternoon. Another sunny summer's day. Once we reached the common, Dad looked at the anti-aircraft guns and marvelled at the number of barrage balloons floating overhead.

'No wonder Hitler hasn't sent any planes over here,' he said. 'Jerry won't try to fly through that lot.'

'Rose calls them flying elephants,' I said.

'They're nice,' Rose replied. 'When the sun shines, they look all silver.'

While Mum and Dad were sitting on a bench, Sheeba ran around the common, chasing me on my bike and generally having fun, until a man in a black suit and a bowler hat came strolling over the grass with a lady.

Sheeba was a really friendly dog and ran over to them, wagging her tail. But the man didn't like it. 'Get away!' he yelled and lashed out with his foot, kicking Sheeba in the ribs so that she yelped and ran off.

When Dad saw what had happened, he leaped to his feet. 'Hey!' he shouted. 'No need for that. She ain't doing any harm.'

The man in the bowler looked across at Dad. 'That's your dog, is it?' he snapped.

'It is,' Dad replied and he called Sheeba to come back and clipped the lead on her collar.

The man glowered at him. 'Then you ought to be ashamed of yourself keeping a German shepherd,' he bellowed. 'It's a Nazi dog. You're a traitor to your country. Any decent Englishman would have had it shot.'

Dad has always been a friendly, even-tempered sort of a bloke – but now I saw his temper flare. His face turned scarlet with anger and he marched up to the man, clenching his fist.

'What did you say?' he asked, staring him in the face.

The man didn't move. 'I said those sort of dogs should be put down. They're Hitler's animals! You're nothing but a traitor!'

That was too much for Dad. He raised his fist and whacked the man in the face, knocking him to the ground where he lay shaking, his nose running with blood.

'Traitor, am I?' yelled Dad, leaning over him. 'Was I a traitor at Dunkirk? Was I a traitor fighting in Belgium to keep people like you safe? Eh, eh?'

Dad was wild. A crazy man. He was out of control.

Mum ran over to him. 'Norman, no!' she called and tried to stop him from hitting the man again. 'Come away!'

But he wouldn't.

Dad raged all the more. 'You in your posh suit and your bowler hat. You know nothing. You've seen nothing. What are you doing for the war? I don't suppose *you're* in the army, are you? No! Your type leaves the dirty work to other people.'

Then the lady stepped in. 'Leave my husband alone!' she screamed. 'He has a job of national importance.'

'Like what?' snapped Dad.

'He works in the bank.'

Dad snorted and raised his fist again, but Mum managed to grab hold of his arm this time and she pulled him away. 'That's enough, Norman. Calm down. Them people are not worth it.'

I'd never seen Dad like that. He didn't even look like my dad. His face was screwed up with anger and he was shaking.

'Come on, Norman,' said Mum quietly. 'Let's go.' She led him away and we all walked home in silence, me wheeling my bike with Sheeba at my heels.

When we got back, Dad went into the garden by himself and sat on the old bench next to the shed, smoking. I wished he wouldn't smoke. Those ciggies only made him cough.

'Go and see if he'll talk to you, Billy,' said Mum, a little nervously. 'Try and cheer him up, darlin'.'

So I went out and sat next to him.

'What is it, Dad?' I said. 'Is it the war?'

For a while he didn't answer. Then he said, 'It's bad, Billy.'

I waited. 'How d'you mean, "Bad"?'

Dad leaned forward and rested his head in his hands. 'Like a nightmare, son. But you never wake up.' He drew on his fag before he spoke again. 'I was over there fighting to keep Hitler out of Britain. I was fighting for you and Rose and your mum. But it's brutal. Strong men suddenly brought down in the mud. Their legs gone. Backs broken. Their lives changed for ever. When I shut my eyes, that's what I see.'

He straightened up and put his arm round my shoulder.

'I'm ashamed of how I behaved today, Billy.' His eyes were full of tears and he wiped one away as it spilled onto his cheek. I'd never seen him cry before. Never.

'A man shouldn't lose control like that. But war changes you. That's the worst of it.'

We were silent for a minute or so and then I said, 'When you were shouting at that man, you mentioned Dunkirk. You weren't there, were you, Dad?'

Slowly he nodded.

'They showed it in the news at the pictures,' I told him. 'I saw it, Dad. But I didn't know you were there. Who rescued you?'

'It was an old man in a fishing boat,' he said, staring into the distance. 'We'd been waiting for days to be taken off that beach – no food and little to drink. All the time we were waiting, German planes were circling overhead, dropping bombs. We thought we were going to die.' He stopped and swallowed and then he reached out for my hand as if he needed help to carry on. 'The beach was a mass of bomb craters... dead soldiers everywhere... smashed vehicles... It was like a scene from hell.' He paused. 'But one old man in a fishing boat saved us. He came across the Channel with hundreds of other boats and saved us – Herbert, Fred and me.'

'He was brave, eh, Dad? I wish I could have rowed a boat to Dunkirk.'

He looked at me, shaking his head. 'But what was it all for, Billy? We were saved then, but Herbert got shot a month later.'

'Is he dead?'

'No. He's in hospital. But he'll never walk again.' Dad was near to tears as he turned and grasped my shoulders. 'I'm thankful you were safe in England, son. More than anything, I want you to stay safe and look after your mum and your sister.' He fixed me with his sad blue eyes, pleading with me. 'Remember, Billy, you're the man of the house now.'

Four

A night in the shelter

We stayed sitting on that bench for some time and, when we went back inside, Dad was looking more like his old self, trying to smile as he walked into the kitchen.

'Spam fritters, mashed potatoes and carrots,' Mum said as she gave Dad a big hug. 'It'll be ready in five minutes.'

Dad sat at the table while Mum served up the fritters and gave Sheeba the leftovers. Dad must have been really hungry because his plate was empty before any of ours.

'Thanks, Ruby, love,' he said, putting down his knife and fork. 'That was delicious.' Then he looked at us, watching us finish our dinners. He didn't say a word. He just smiled as if he wanted to remember this moment to take back with him. Something to treasure like a photo he could look at over and over again while he was away.

When we'd finished eating, Dad slapped his hand on the table and the silence was broken.

'How about another slice of your birthday cake for afters, Billy? Is that all right?'

I grinned and nodded. 'That sounds like a good idea, Dad.'

Mum jumped up, fetched the cake out of the kitchen cabinet and put it on the table. 'Cut your dad an extra big slice, Billy. It'll do him good. Don't let anybody say I neglect my husband! While you're in this house, Norman Wilson, you'll eat like a king.'

That made Dad laugh. 'And you're my queen, Ruby Wilson,' he said, and Mum blushed.

At eight o'clock that night the siren started wailing.

'Oh, not Moaning Minnie again,' said Mum. 'It's such a horrible noise.'

Dad raised his eyebrows. 'Ruby! That's a warning that there's going to be an air raid. Jerry's only across the Channel, you know.'

'There won't be no air raid, Norman,' said Mum. 'It's only a practice. They have them every now and then. We don't take any notice, do we, kids?'

Dad didn't look pleased. 'If that's the case, we'll have a practice of our own. Get your things and we'll be off to the shelter.'

Mum sighed. 'Then we'd better put our coats on,' she said. 'It'll get cold later on.'

Just to please Dad we all hurried to the Anderson shelter carrying our gas masks and blankets. I had a copy of *The Beano* with me and Rose took Goldilocks as usual. Mum went inside and lit some candles, then we followed. But I didn't much like it in there. For one thing there was a nasty smell of damp earth and drains.

'Shut the door, Billy,' said Dad. 'Keep old Hitler out, eh?'

'He ain't here, Norman,' Mum insisted. 'I keep telling you – it's just a practice.'

'Then why hasn't the All Clear sounded? How do you know they're not expecting Nazi planes to come over?'

The shelter wasn't a nice place to be and we all felt miserable. But Dad had brought his banjo with him and he played 'Pack Up Your Troubles in Your Old Kit Bag', which made us feel better and we all sang except Rose, who was sitting on the edge of the bunk, clutching Goldilocks and whimpering.

'What is it, my lovely?' asked Dad, putting his banjo on the ground and lifting Rose onto his knee.

She clung to him and murmured, 'It's that nasty man. I'm frightened.'

'What nasty man?'

'That Hitler man. He's outside in our garden.'

Dad hugged her and said, 'No, he's not, sweetheart. He's miles and miles away.'

'But he might come and hurt us.'

Dad peeled her arms from round his neck. 'I want to show you something, Rose,' he said and he put his hand in his jacket. 'This is something special. It's magic.'

He pulled out a silver pocket watch and held it up by its chain so that it twirled and glistened in the candlelight.

'Mum gave it to me,' he said. 'It belonged to her grandfather, see, so it's very, very old. She had my name engraved on it, and she gave it to me for my birthday, didn't you, love?'

Mum smiled and nodded as he handed the watch to Rose.

'When the war started, I took it with me to remind me of my family and how lucky I was to have you all.'

Rose held the watch and frowned. 'It's broken,' she said.

It was true. The glass was cracked and the back was badly dented.

'Well,' Dad continued, 'let me tell you a story. One day I was in a country called Belgium with my mates Fred and Herbert. The Germans were shooting at us. We were trying to keep our heads down, but bullets were flying left, right and centre. Then one of the bullets flew right at me and struck me in the chest.'

Mum gasped. 'Norman!'

'Did it hurt?' asked Rose.

'No, because the bullet hit my silver pocket watch.'

I leaned forward and stared at the dent caused by the bullet.

'Cor!' I said. 'So the pocket watch saved you, Dad?'

'It did. Now it's my good luck charm,' he said. 'I always keep it with me, see. It's a kind of magic.' He closed Rose's hand over the watch. 'You hold it, pickle. Hold it tight and it'll keep you safe.'

Rose clutched it to her chest and snuggled up to Dad like a chick with a mother hen. Once she'd closed her eyes, Dad put her onto the bottom bunk and tucked a blanket round her. Sheeba jumped up, too, curling up against her legs and soon they were both fast asleep.

Five

Waving goodbye

'So what did you think of your first night in the shelter?' Dad asked as we sat round the table in the kitchen waiting for breakfast.

'That was the worst night's sleep I've ever had, Norman,' Mum told him as she filled the kettle to make a pot of tea. 'It felt ever so damp.'

'You'll get used to it, darlin'. I've slept in worse places than that these past months.'

She turned and stared at Dad. 'But why do we have to get used to it? There ain't been no bombing in Balham.'

'Listen to me, Ruby. Hitler's invaded the Channel Islands. It might not be long before he starts bombing London. It's only up the road from here. What if he drops bombs on Balham?'

'Oh, it won't happen,' said Mum without looking at Dad. 'They just want to frighten us.' She reached over and took a loaf out of the kitchen cabinet.

Dad stood up. 'No, Ruby, you've got to believe me,' he said, taking hold of Mum's hands and looking straight into her eyes.

'It's getting serious, love. Now I want you to promise me something.'

'What?'

'I want you to promise that, if things get bad over here, you'll go to my folks in Yorkshire.'

Mum pulled her hands away and started cutting the bread into slices, pretending she hadn't heard.

'Ruby,' Dad said. 'Are you listening?'

Mum spun round. 'I don't want to go. Your mother always thought you should never have left the farm to marry a silly blonde like me.'

'No, Ruby! It's not true.'

'She'll think I can't manage. But I can! I'll show her. We can manage just fine. I've done all right up to now, haven't I?'

Dad ran his fingers through his hair, exasperated by what Mum had said. 'But the kids aren't getting an education here. If they went up to Yorkshire they'd be able to go to school and there'd be things for them to do on the farm. They always like it when we go up there.'

Rose didn't miss a thing. 'Are we going to stay with Gran and Grandad?' she asked. 'They've got lambs and chickens. Oh, can we, Mum? Can we?'

'Now see what you've done, Norman,' Mum said, sniffing away a tear. 'I want to look after my kids myself.'

'But you'd be going with them,' Dad argued.

She slammed the kettle on the stove and turned to look at him. 'No, I can't go. I've work to do. I've got a job and I can't let people down.'

He glared at her in disbelief. 'What did you say? You've got a job?'

Mum blushed. 'I have.'

'Whatever for? Ain't you got enough to do looking after our Billy and Rose?'

'They're well looked after. They go next door to Iris Scott while I'm at work,' she said. 'And...I need the money, Norman. The kids are growing. You don't think of that. They need new shoes and coats for the winter.' She snatched the biscuit tin out of the kitchen cabinet and rattled it. 'There's nine bob in here, that's all! And some of that's for the milkman. It's all I've got to last the week.'

Mum and Dad didn't often argue, but this was becoming a real barney so I took Sheeba and Rose into the garden to get out of the way. But when we went back in, they were still at it.

'Your mother's working at Lodey's garage,' Dad said to me as if I didn't know. 'I'm not happy, Billy.'

'It's the war, Dad,' I said. 'Things are different.'

Dad shook his head. 'A man should be able to look after his family, son. His wife shouldn't be going out to work.' He stormed upstairs and came back clutching four pound notes. 'You take these, Ruby. I got paid when I landed. This should keep you going for a bit.'

Mum took the money and kissed him on the cheek. 'Thank you, Norman. But it's not just the money. You see, you go abroad and fight for our country, but all I do is stay at home. It's only right I should do something to help out.'

Dad scratched his head. 'But what if a bomb drops on Lodey's Garage, Ruby? All that petrol. BOOM! You'd go sky high. You wouldn't be able to look after the kids then, would you?'

Mum gave a huge sigh and looked down at the floor, shaking her head from side to side. 'I don't know what to think,' she said. 'We haven't had any bombs round here and it's been safe enough what with the barrage balloons and that.' She blew her nose and wiped her eyes. 'Look, Norman, I'm sorry. I know you're worried about us. If you want me to, I'll write to your mother and ask her if she'll have us.'

'Why not ring her?' said Dad. 'They've got a telephone at the farm.'

Mum sighed. 'But it costs a lot for a trunk call.'

Dad lowered his voice. 'Ruby! There's enough money for that. And there's a telephone box on the corner of Rossiter Road.'

'All right. I'll do it after you've gone, Norman. I promise. But I don't want to waste a single minute till then. It's your last day, let's not quarrel no more.'

Dad put his arms round her. 'All right, darlin'. But I want you to promise that if that siren goes off you'll sleep in the shelter – just till you go to Yorkshire.'

'Right, Norman. I promise.'

'Thanks,' he said. 'Now I can go back with an easy mind.'

The rest of the day went quickly and it wasn't long before Dad went upstairs to put on his uniform.

'We're going with you to the railway station this time,' said

Mum. Dad tried to protest. He didn't like saying goodbye, but this time Mum insisted.

'I give in,' he said. 'Right. Let's be off then.'

Rose was really excited. She loved trains. Not the underground kind. She liked those big noisy ones that puffed out lots of steam – the kind that took us up to Yorkshire to see Gran and Grandad.

Dad carried her on his shoulders onto the platform. Then he set her down and gave her a goodbye kiss before giving Mum an even bigger one. When he pulled away Mum was crying.

He turned to me, shook my hand and said, 'You look after these two, Billy. Remember what I said – you're the man of the house now.'

I felt very grown-up, but very sad at the same time cos I didn't want Dad to go. My stomach started to churn and I almost started blubbing – but Balham boys don't cry. So I just said, 'Don't worry, Dad. I'll look after 'em.'

Rose didn't understand what was going on. She must have thought we were all going on the train with Dad, and when he said, 'I've got to go now,' she burst out sobbing and Mum had to keep hold of her hand to stop her running after him as he climbed on board.

The train was crowded with men in khaki uniform and some in blue. Dad stood in the corridor with some other soldiers and, when all the doors were slammed shut, he leaned out of the window and waved to us.

'Write to me, won't you?' he shouted. 'Billy, look after my banjo. See if you can learn to play it while I'm away.'

'I will, Dad,' I yelled back.

We stepped well away from the train and stood there waving. But before we knew it, Rose had slipped from Mum's grip and run towards the train shouting, 'Dad! Dad!' waving the silver pocket watch in her little fist and holding it up for Dad to take.

'You keep it, Rose,' he shouted over the noise of the engine.

Rose shook her head. 'No! No! It's for you, Dad,' she sobbed. 'You have it to keep you safe.'

Dad smiled, reached down and took it from her. The guard blew the whistle and, when the train began to pull away, he held the pocket watch close to his chest, his eyes full of tears as he waved us goodbye.

Six

The day everything changed

Mum waited till the next morning to go to the telephone box and ring Gran.

'I don't like asking her to look after us,' she told me before she left, 'but I promised Dad I'd do it.'

Rose was next door playing with the twins and I did some digging in the garden while I waited for Mum. But when she came back, it wasn't good news.

'Grandma was in a real state, Billy. Your grandad's very ill.'

'No!' I said, dropping the fork on the ground. 'But he's never had a day's illness in his life. What's wrong? It's not serious, is it?'

'He's been taken to hospital,' Mum said. 'He's had a heart attack.'

I felt sick thinking of Grandad lying in a hospital bed. He was always so fit and strong. What if he didn't get better? We'd had such great times on the farm. Fetching in the hay. Feeding the chickens. I couldn't imagine it without him.

Mum put her hand on my shoulder. 'I'm sorry, Billy. I know

it's bad news but, in the circumstances, I couldn't ask Grandma if we could come and stay, could I? She's got enough to think about.'

I felt so bad about Grandad, I'd almost forgotten about our plans to leave Balham.

'We'll just carry on as we are until he's better, eh?' said Mum. 'It might not be long.'

Mum went back to work at the garage and Mrs Scott kept her eye on us during the day. I went and queued up at the butcher's to get our meat ration, and although fish wasn't rationed I still had to queue at the fishmonger's. Every day seemed like one big queue.

When I wasn't queuing, Rose and me pushed Mrs Scott's babies out for some fresh air. At night, if the siren went off, we slept in the shelter – not because we wanted to, but because we'd promised Dad.

Then one day the Nazis dropped bombs on London and Liverpool and Birmingham, killing loads of people. Everyone was shocked. Buildings were destroyed and the docks had been set on fire. It must have been terrible for all those living near.

Still no bombs fell on Balham.

But on the seventh of September things changed for thousands of people – including us. That day, Mum had taken the afternoon off work and we'd gone down to the common to give Sheeba a good run. We'd got home about half past three. Mum started making a fish pie and I went out and dug up some potatoes.

I'd just put them in a bucket ready to take into the kitchen when Moaning Minnie started up and I ran back into the house.

Mum looked worried. 'That's early. It's not even dark yet,' she said. 'Come on, Billy. Get your things and we'll go down to the shelter.'

Rose grabbed Goldilocks and we were off. By then we were used to the shelter, even though Mum didn't see the point of it. But that day was different. I could feel it. Something bad was going to happen.

We sat on the edge of the bunks pretending that this was just another false alarm, waiting for the All Clear to sound. But it didn't come. Instead I heard planes in the distance. Not British planes. This was the noise of Hitler's Luftwaffe – hundreds of planes, sounding like a swarm of bees in the distance, and getting louder until they swooped overhead filling the air with a deafening roar. The ack-ack guns on the common fired continuously into the sky and I could feel the ground vibrating under my feet. Then the shelter began to shake.

I was so scared that I started to tremble and the hairs at the back of my neck stood on end. All this time, Rose was clinging tight to Mum.

The first wave of planes passed over then I heard the *crump, crump, crump* as bombs fell and exploded in the distance. And just when I thought that was over and done with, the next wave came and the guns set off again. It was like a nightmare – a terrible nightmare – and sweat broke out on my forehead. But this was no nightmare. I was wide awake and it was real. It was the war Dad had warned us about.

Mum was talking in a very loud, very cheerful voice. But I could see that she was frightened and just trying to hide it.

'What a noise!' she said to Rose. 'My goodness I'm glad we've got this shelter. It's nice and cosy, ain't it?'

Wave after wave of bombers came over heading for London. I thought they'd never stop. And they didn't. For the rest of the day and into the night they kept coming. We weren't a big church-going family – apart from Christmas and Easter – but that night Mum got down on her knees and she prayed and prayed to anyone who'd listen. 'Stop them! Oh, please, please stop them! Keep my family safe!'

By ten o'clock, she was exhausted and she lay on the bunk, wrapping her arms round Rose until they both fell asleep.

I closed my eyes, but I couldn't sleep for all the noise of planes and ack-ack guns. So I climbed off the bunk, pushed the door open a crack and squeezed through into the garden. I stared up at the black night sky, but when I turned and looked towards London there was no blackness there. Over the city the sky was blood red, lit up by flames as buildings burned. Dozens of German planes, like a great flock of ravens, were heading for London, silhouetted against the scarlet sky. I saw it! I saw it with my own eyes but I couldn't believe what was happening.

That was the beginning of the war for me. The All Clear

didn't sound till six o'clock in the morning and it was the longest and worst raid of them all.

The morning after that terrible raid, Mrs Scott called to Mum over the fence. 'I've just heard on the wireless. They say the Nazis are trying to flatten London. A lot of people were killed last night.'

Mum held up her hand. 'I don't want to hear about it, Iris,' she said. 'I won't have a wireless in our house. It makes me feel miserable and I don't believe half the things they say.'

'Well, if that's how you feel, Ruby,' Mrs Scott replied.

'My Norman doesn't want us to stay here,' Mum said. 'I'm going to phone his mother again, see if Grandad's any better. Then we'll be going to Yorkshire away from it all.'

She went into the kitchen and took some money out of the biscuit tin. 'I want you to come with me, Billy, to phone Gran,' she said, sounding quite nervous, I thought. 'She'll want to have a chat with you. I expect.'

So we went together to Rossiter Road while Rose stayed with Mrs Scott. She didn't mind because she liked playing with the babies.

When we reached the phone box, we both managed to squeeze inside. Mum spoke to the operator then put the coins in the slot. When Gran answered Mum pressed button A to let the coins drop and then she passed me the handset to talk to her.

'Hello, Gran. It's Billy.'

'Well it's lovely to hear you, Billy,' she said. 'I expect you're wanting to know how Grandad is.'

'Is he out of hospital?' I asked.

'Not yet, Billy. But he's coming home soon and he'll have to sleep downstairs. He'll need some good food and plenty of peace and quiet.'

Mum held out her hand for the receiver and I passed it over.

'There was some terrible bombings in London last night,' she told Gran. 'Have you heard about it?'

'I've been too busy to listen to the news, Ruby. I've got the farm to run as well as going to the hospital. I'm worn out, honestly! What about the bombing? Has there been any near you?'

'No, but—'

'You've got a shelter, haven't you?'

'Yes. Norman built us one of them Anderson shelters.'

'That's what I thought. My Norman's always been good with his hands – just like his father. Norman would have made a grand farmer.' She sighed and then she went on, 'Anyway, I'm glad they're not bombing Balham. It's nice to know you're safe. I'll have to get on, Ruby. A neighbour's coming to help me get the bed downstairs for when Arthur comes home. I've got that much to do, I don't know where to start. But thank you for telephoning. It's very nice of you to worry about my poor Arthur.'

When Mum finally replaced the receiver, she looked defeated.

'We can't go up to Yorkshire,' she said. 'Not with Grandad being so ill. But we can manage for a bit longer, can't we?'

41

I said, 'Course we can, Mum.' But I was hoping that Grandad would get well soon. With things getting worse in London, we needed to get away.

After that terrible raid, the siren sounded every night and, just as Dad feared, bombs started falling on Balham. The Odeon Cinema was flattened and some shops on Balham High Road were damaged. We heard that people had been killed. One family – the Bingleys – we knew quite well. Little Benny used to go to my school. He was only seven. They hadn't gone into a shelter that night and one of the bombs landed on their house. A direct hit, it was. I felt sick thinking how they had died and that it could happen to us: me, Rose and Mum. Dad was right – we had to sleep in the shelter to be safe.

Mum gave up work at the garage. 'I don't want to be away from home. I want to be here looking after you two, don't I?' She was frightened that a raid might happen in the middle of the day – but it never did after that first one.

Our life developed a sort of pattern. Moaning Minnie would sound most evenings and we'd all get ready to go down to the shelter just like we'd promised Dad. We'd collect our things and Mum would kiss Dad's photo on the mantelpiece. When the bombing was really bad I played Dad's banjo to drown out the noise. Not that I could play properly. It was just a sort-of twangy-twang – but it made Rose laugh, which was much better than seeing her cry.

By October, the weather had turned cold and it rained a lot. When water seeped into the shelter Mum did her best to stop it but some rain dripped onto our beds and soaked the blankets.

She tried to be brave about it and laughed it off as an adventure. 'We won't let that Hitler beat us, will we?' she'd say. But several times I heard her crying when she thought I was asleep.

One day, she told us that Mrs Scott's shelter's was leaking like ours. 'She's going down Balham tube station tonight,' she said. 'So I think we'll go, too, shall we? It'll be nice and quiet. You can't hear the bombs down there so we'll get a good night's sleep.'

'But when are we going to Gran's?' Rose asked. 'You said we were going soon.'

'I'll ring Gran again and see how Grandad is. So be a good girl till then.'

'Is Sheeba coming with us?' I asked.

'She can go up to Yorkshire with us but she can't come down the tube station. They won't allow animals.'

'Why not?' Rose asked. 'Where will she stay?'

'We'll leave her in the shelter. She'll be safe there and I'll put her rug on the bottom bunk bed so she won't get wet.'

That was what we planned. We would go the to the tube station, which was deep underground. We thought we would be safe.

Seven

An underground shelter

Before Moaning Minnie started up that night, we settled
Sheeba in the Anderson shelter.

'We'll be back in the morning,' said Rose, and she gave her
some mashed potato and an extra hug.

Mum kissed Dad's photo and said, 'Sleep tight, Norman.
Keep safe,' like she always did. Then we set off down Fernlea
Road carrying our bundles of blankets and pillows. I held
Mum's torch to help us find our way through the blackout.
She'd covered the end with tissue paper so that it wasn't
too bright.

'Shine it down at the pavement, Billy,' she told me. 'We don't
want them German bombers seeing us, do we?'

Everywhere was pitch-black cos the street lights had been
turned off and everyone's windows were covered in blackout
curtains. The edges of the pavements had been painted white
– so that helped a bit. But you still had to be careful. It was
easy to trip up and loads of accidents happened cos people
couldn't see very well. Cars bumped into walls. Buses smashed
into lorries. And people got knocked down crossing the road.

It was very dangerous.

We all carried a blanket and, as well as that, I took some *Beano*s and Dad's banjo – just in case one of Hitler's bombs landed on our house and squashed it. Rose had Goldilocks tucked under her arm, but Mum carried the weirdest thing of all – the tin box where she kept her curlers and a lipstick.

When we reached the tube station it was tricky carrying our stuff down the steps to the platform. Rose wasn't careful enough and she tripped over her blanket. Mum flung out her arms to stop Rose falling headfirst but, as she did, she dropped her box, the lid burst open and the curlers fell out, bouncing down the steps and onto the platform. We spent the next ten minutes picking them up and putting them back in the box. But we never did find Mum's lipstick.

The platform of Balham tube station looked like a bigger version of our Anderson shelter at home with its curved roof and curved walls. We'd been there loads of times to catch the underground trains into London, but we'd never been there to sleep. The air was thick with a sickly, sweaty smell and I thought it must be coming from the people who slept there, crammed together every night.

But there was one good thing. The underground was brightly lit with plenty of electric lights so I'd be able to read my *Beanos*.

Some people had already put down their blankets and were sitting on the platform, reading newspapers or playing cards. But before we could settle ourselves, a train came rushing through the station bringing a blast of air and deafening us

45

with its noise. People on the train were looking out of the windows staring at us as if we were animals in a zoo.

'You told us it would be quiet down here, Mum,' I said as I dropped my blanket onto the platform. 'How are we going to sleep? The noise of them trains makes my teeth rattle.'

She laughed. 'Don't you worry, Billy. They won't be running all night. It'll be quiet soon, you'll see. And we won't hear the bombs.'

As I sat on my blanket, I noticed someone further down the platform, standing up and waving to us.

'It's Mrs Scott,' said Mum and waved back.

'Come over 'ere, Ruby,' Mrs Scott shouted. 'I've saved you a space.'

Mum seemed keen to go, so we picked up our belongings and set off. It wasn't easy, edging along the platform, stepping over legs and in between feet, but we finally got to the place where Mrs Scott was sitting.

Her twins were about nine months old and Mum always made a great fuss of them. Dad said babies made a lot of noise and a lot of work – but Mum said they were lovely.

'Nice of you to keep a spot for us,' said Mum when we reached Mrs Scott. 'I'll be able you help you with the babies.'

While Mum and her friend were chatting, Rose and me arranged our blankets, put our gas masks on top and I put the banjo in the middle where it wouldn't get knocked. We sat and watched people flooding into the tube station, and before we knew it, it was full and we were jammed together like sardines in a tin. There was even a family sitting on the steps.

A few more trains passed through, but they soon stopped running and then people started a sing-song. They sang 'It's a Long Way to Tipperary' and 'Pack Up Your Troubles in Your Old Kit Bag' while some of the little 'uns ran about playing hide-and-seek.

I would have been happy reading my *Beanos*, but Rose wanted to show me what she'd found. 'Come and see, Billy,' she said and she tugged my hand and took me to the edge of the platform.

'Look!' she said, pointing down to the track. 'Mice. Lots of them.'

Sure enough, a number of small grey mice with long tails were running between the rail tracks. There were so many that I made up a game to keep Rose happy. We both had to choose a mouse and then watch to see whose mouse ran the furthest before it disappeared. Rose's mice were best. Mine kept running into a gap between the bricks in the wall.

When we'd had enough, we went back and sat next to Mum, who was putting curlers in her hair.

Mrs Scott was on the other side giving the babies a bottle. 'You keep yourself looking smart, Ruby,' I heard her say to Mum.

'Norman wouldn't like it if I went scruffy, Iris. There's no need, is there – just because there's a war on.'

'I bet you miss working at the garage, don't you?'

'I do. I liked putting the petrol in the cars and chatting to the customers. Not that there's many cars about now.'

'No,' said Mrs Scott. 'People have shut 'em away now that

petrol's rationed. Shame, ain't it?'

Rose, wanting some attention, climbed over Mum's legs and squeezed between the two of them. 'We're going to stay with Gran and Grandad,' she said, looking up at Mrs Scott. 'They've got a farm and I'm going to help Grandad feed the lambs.'

I left them to get on with their gossip, leaned against the tiled wall and pulled *The Beano* out of my pocket. Sitting next to me was an old man with a grey beard and a wrinkly forehead. He reminded me of Grandad, especially when he smiled. He told me his name was Tommy. 'These are my neighbours, Walter and Mary,' he said, introducing me to a couple sitting next to him.

I nodded and said hello, then Tommy leaned over. 'That's a fine looking instrument you've got there,' he said, looking at the banjo on the blanket.

'It's my dad's,' I said. 'He's away in the army.'

'Can you play it, son?'

'Not much. But I want to learn. Dad said he'd teach me after the war.'

'I used to play a bit in my day. I'll teach you now, if you like,' said Tommy. 'It'll pass the time nicely.' I handed him the banjo and he started to play it.

'You're good,' I said as I watched his fingers fly across the strings, playing a jolly tune that made me smile. That night, Tommy gave me my first lesson. He showed me where to place the fingers of my left hand and how to strum my other hand quickly across the strings. I think I did quite well.

'If you practise when you're at home,' Tommy told me, 'I'll give you another lesson tomorrow night. By the time your dad comes back on leave, you'll be able to play a tune for him.'

I liked that idea and hoped that one day I would be able to play as well as Dad.

Tommy's friend Walter was reading the paper. 'What's the news?' Tommy asked.

'They're saying Hitler sent a hundred and sixty-five planes over London last night.'

'Gordon Bennett!' said Tommy. 'What happened?'

'A lot of damage, so they say, and Buckingham Palace was hit. It's disgusting.'

'What about the King and Queen?'

'Nobody hurt, thank the Lord.' And with that, he turned over the page.

By then, Mum had all her curlers in place and was holding one of the babies, rocking her to sleep. Rose was lying down under the blanket cuddling Goldilocks, and Tommy had fallen asleep, his chin on his chest, snoring gently.

Gradually the underground grew quiet as people stopped talking and everybody settled down for the night, lying like sausages in a pan, squashed up together.

But safe.

Eight

A great explosion

Mum rang Gran a couple more times.

'Grandad's at home, but he's not very well yet,' Mum told me. 'Gran's looking after him, but I think she's finding it hard work keeping him calm and quiet.'

'When can we go to Yorkshire?' I asked. 'I want to see him.'

'Give it a week or two,' she said. 'Grandad should be better by then.'

Over those weeks, we got used to walking past bombed out shops on the Balham High Road. We'd forgotten the time when we could buy food without queuing for it.

Every night we went down to the tube station and Tommy would give me another lesson on the banjo. He made me play chords over and over until I got them just right and soon I was good enough to play 'Rule Britannia' while Tommy sang the words. Dad would be really pleased with me and I couldn't wait to show him what I could do.

But down in the tube station we never got a proper night's sleep. It was uncomfortable lying on the hard platform and I longed for my own bed with Sheeba sleeping nearby. In the underground there was always someone coughing, snoring or crying and when morning came we were still tired. We yawned a lot during the day and Mum had dark circles under her eyes. She must have been worrying about us being safe. Worrying about feeding us. Worrying about Dad fighting the Nazis. But she always said, 'We'll never give in to that Hitler. Never! We'll all stick together and we'll win through.'

One afternoon, Mum heard that the local butcher had sausages for sale. She dashed off to try and get some, but by the time she came home it was almost dark and she hadn't managed to buy any.

'Sold out!' she said. 'I got back as quick as I could, but it's too late to cook anything now.' She opened the door of the kitchen cabinet and reached for a tin. 'We'll take some bread and Spam down the tube station, eh? But we'd best hurry before Moaning Minnie starts.'

While Mum gathered the food together and made a flask of tea, Rose and me took Sheeba to the Anderson shelter and gave her some leftover mash and gravy. We topped up the water in her dish and she jumped onto the bottom bunk, ready to settle down for the night.

'See you tomorrow, girl,' said Rose, and Sheeba whined as we went out and shut the door behind us. I hated leaving her alone down there. She must have been so scared listening to the bombs exploding, wondering whether we'd be coming back. I wished we could take her down the tube but they were very strict about no animals. Every morning when we let her

51

out she was really pleased to see us and leaped up, wagging her tail so hard it whipped at our legs and almost knocked us over. But now we had to say goodbye again.

That night, as I shut the door of the shelter, the siren began to wail. It was earlier than usual.

'Come on!' Mum shouted from the kitchen door. 'Quick as you can.'

We grabbed our coats, blankets and gas masks. Then, with only the dim light of the torch to show us our way, the three of us ran down the road in the blackout, careful not to trip over any rubble lying around. The noise of the air-raid siren filled the air and was so deafening we couldn't hear each other speak.

We ran as fast as we could, thinking that the German planes might come over any minute. By the time we reached the tube station there was a queue – longer than ever – of people waiting to go in. They shuffled forward down the steps and we followed, with Mum insisting that we held onto the rail so we wouldn't fall.

When we finally reached the platform, we couldn't go to our usual space in the middle. It was already full.

'Never mind,' said Mum. 'We'll settle ourselves at this end instead.' And we all dropped our blankets onto the platform just a few yards from the steps.

While Rose and me were getting comfortable, Mum spotted Mrs Scott not far away standing up with one of the babies in her arms.

'Iris!' Mum called. 'We're here!'

Mrs Scott waved back then Mum turned to us and said, 'We can't sit next to Iris tonight, the platform's too crowded. But I'll go over and have a word with her. Baby Grace hasn't been well all day. She's got a bad chest. You stay here, Billy, and look after your sister.'

'I want to come, too,' said Rose.

'Not tonight, darlin',' said Mum. 'Play a nice game with Billy. I won't be long.'

I had a bag of marbles in my pocket. 'Come on, Rose. Let's play marbles, eh?' I gave her the bag. 'You share them out – half for me and half for you.'

While Mum stepped over people's legs to reach Mrs Scott, I found a piece of chalk in my pocket and drew a circle on the platform so we could play. We had just rolled the first marbles when a familiar voice called, 'Hello, Billy. Got time for another lesson?'

I turned and saw Tommy. I hadn't noticed him when we arrived. But there he was with his friends, Walter and Mary, sitting just a few feet away.

'Thanks, Tommy. I'd like that,' I said. 'I'll have to wait till Mum comes back. She's gone to see her friend.' Then I suddenly remembered – in my rush to leave the house, I'd left Dad's banjo behind.

But Tommy smiled when I told him. 'We all forget things sometimes,' he said. 'Never mind. There's always tomorrow.' And he picked up his newspaper and settled down to read.

By the time Mum came back, Rose had won three of my best marbles.

'Look what I got, Mum!' she said, holding out her hand. 'I'm good at marbles, aren't I, Billy?'

Mum laughed and gave her a kiss. 'Sorry I was so long,' she said. 'Baby Grace has a high temperature and she won't stop crying. Poor mite. Her little face is bright pink. It's not right babies being in a place like this when they're poorly.'

'I don't like it down here,' said Rose, wrinkling her nose. 'It's smelly. I want to go to Gran's. Can we go?'

'Soon, darlin'. When Grandad's better.' Mum put her arm round Rose's shoulder. 'But you have fun with Billy, don't you? You get to stay up late and play games. That's good, ain't it?'

'I want to stay in our house,' Rose complained.

I felt the same way. I wanted to sleep in my own bed. I wanted my friends to come back to Balham and my dad to be at home with us. Some days I even wanted to go back to school.

'We can't always have what we want, love,' Mum said sadly and I guessed she was thinking about Dad.

Mum sat down and held Rose tight, rocking her backwards and forward until she fell asleep clutching her doll.

It was strange that night. Usually people sang to cheer themselves up. But nobody was singing. It was as if life was getting too hard to make the effort. Instead they talked in low voices or played cards. The only loud noise was baby Grace's crying, which echoed down the tunnels and couldn't be stopped no matter how much Mrs Scott tried.

'The poor thing isn't well. She needs some medicine,' said Mum. 'I'll go over and help Iris for a bit.'

Mum lifted Rose off her knee, put her onto the blanket and covered her up. 'Keep an eye on her, will you, Billy?' she said. 'I won't be long.'

I watched Mum step along the platform to Mrs Scott, take baby Grace in her arms and begin to rock her gently backwards and forward.

Then it happened.

Suddenly, quite out of the blue, there was a bang so loud and terrifying I thought my eardrums had burst. The noise was like a great explosion over our heads and for a few seconds my brain stopped working and I couldn't think what was going on. I only knew that it was something very serious.

Nine

Chaos

After that first terrifying bang, people sat up and looked in the direction of the noise. A crack appeared in the ceiling further down the platform. It was small at first. Then I watched, my mouth gaping open, as the crack split into two then four, six, ten and spread like a great spider across the roof of the tunnel. Was this an earthquake? I thought. I'd learned about them at school. But they didn't happen in London, did they?

Everyone on the platform stared up at the ceiling for what seemed like ages – but it was probably just a few seconds before the cracks split wide open. Water and rubble burst through the hole, pouring down onto everything below.

Then the lights went out and there was nothing but blackness and noise.

Terrified, I reached out for the tiled wall, glad to feel something steady. I bent down and felt Rose's blanket and I heard her scream my name. 'Billy! Billy! I'm frightened.'

I felt her hand touch mine and I grabbed hold of it and pulled her upright as the water rushed around my feet.

'Come on, Rose!' I yelled. 'We've got to get out of here.'

By then, people were screaming and calling to their children, lost in the darkness.

I shouted, too. 'Mum! Mum! Where are you?'

But it was hopeless. I couldn't make myself heard cos the tunnel was filled with noise – water rushing, people shouting. Every sound echoed and grew even louder. And then – as if we hadn't suffered enough – an avalanche of mud and stones burst through that hole in the ceiling and onto our heads.

There were more ear-piercing cries as everyone panicked, not knowing where to turn. How to get to safety. Then, one by one, tiny spots of light appeared as people turned on their torches. They looked like stars bouncing on the black water, as it raced along the platform taking gravel and grit with it. It swirled around my ankles, stones scraping against my legs.

I squeezed Rose's hand and tugged her in the direction of the steps. 'This way. Come on, Rose!' I yelled. But she held back crying, 'I want Mum! Where is she?'

Suddenly, someone grabbed hold of me.

'You've got to move, Billy!' It was Tommy.

He swept Rose into his arms. 'I've got your sister. Now grab hold of my jacket. We've got to stay together. Come on.'

'I want Mum,' wailed Rose.

'She'll be following us,' Tommy assured her as we tried to move ahead.

By then people were frantically pushing and shoving towards the exit. For a second, as I was knocked against the wall, I let go of Tommy's coat and I thought I was lost. But somehow I managed to grab hold of it again and we began to move forward.

Rose was still crying out for Mum. But there was nothing I could do. I could hardly see anything in the dark. I just hoped we'd meet up once we got outside. That's what I prayed for.

The water was stinking, ankle-deep and rising fast. We dragged our legs slowly through it, bumping along with the crowd. We were jammed so tight together that I was afraid of losing Rose and Tommy. I was afraid of slipping off the platform into the water on the line below. It was lucky we weren't far from the stairs that night or we wouldn't have stood a chance of getting out.

As I put my foot on the first step I felt a surge of relief. Escape was in sight. We were going to get out and breathe fresh air again. With the second step, I was clear of the water but after that the climb to the exit was so frightening and slow. People were jostling each other in their attempt to get out. There must have been thirty, forty, fifty people in front of us on those steps. If someone slipped backwards we'd all fall like a pack of cards.

Tommy turned his head and called over his shoulder. 'You all right, Billy? Just keep going and we'll soon be out.'

Step by step we went, pressed on every side. It seemed a terrible long way. But when we reached the top I was relieved to feel wind on my face.

Out in the open there wasn't the calm I had hoped for. Everything in front of the tube station was in chaos. It was terrifying. The air was filled with thick black smoke, and flames leaped from nearby buildings. The road was crowded with frightened people shouting and sobbing, wandering about in a daze. We pushed our way onto the pavement. Tommy put Rose down and we stood looking around for Mum. But we couldn't see her.

ARP wardens were trying to control the crowds, shooing people away from the entrance of the tube station. 'Make room for people to get out,' they shouted. 'Go home. Get into your Anderson shelters. Don't stay here.'

Rose turned to Tommy and clung to him. 'Where's my mum?' she said – although she could hardly speak for sobbing. 'I want Mum. Will you go and find her? Please!'

He picked her up and kissed her on the cheek. 'She'll come soon, Rose. We'll just have to wait here for a bit longer.'

When Mum didn't arrive, Tommy called one of the wardens over. 'Will you look after these two?' he asked. 'I've got to go and find their mother.'

But the warden said he couldn't. He had too many people to look after. 'Take 'em home,' he said before he turned away and disappeared into the crowd.

Tommy looked anxious. 'Do you think you could wait round the corner, Billy, while I go and look for your mum? I want to see if Walter and Mary need any help, too. They're not so steady on their legs.'

I said I'd look after Rose. Then Tommy found us a safe place with an overhanging roof, not far from the entrance to the station and I promised we'd stay there while he went back inside. 'But what if Mum's looking for us?' I said. 'She might not see us here.'

'If I see her, I'll tell her where you are. All right?'

I nodded, though I didn't like the idea of us being by ourselves.

'I'll be as quick as I can,' Tommy said. 'You won't move, will you?'

As he hurried away, I looked down at Rose. 'We'll be all right,' I said. 'Tommy'll find Mum.' And she sniffed and clung onto my jacket.

We were soaking wet and cold – not to mention really scared – as we stood there pressed close to the wall. I wrapped my arms round Rose and held her tight. She was shaking from the top of her head right down to her toes. This was the worst nightmare I could imagine. As we clung together, German planes roared overhead dropping their cargo of bombs. The sky was alight with flames from burning buildings and I was terrified by what I saw. I wanted to run away, but I knew that I had to stay calm and look after my sister. I pressed her face to my chest so she wouldn't see the fires. But that didn't block out the noise of the explosions and it didn't stop her shaking.

'I want Mum,' she wailed. 'Where is she, Billy?'

'I expect she's on her way,' I said, when really I wanted to yell, 'Mum! Why aren't you here? Come and look after us.' But Balham boys don't do that.

Crowds pressed round us hurrying to find shelter. We didn't move. We'd promised Tommy to stay here and we would – until Mum came.

The bombing stopped, for the time being at least. All around us was the clanging of fire engines and whooping of ambulances as they arrived on the scene. We stood on that corner for ages, frightened, waiting and wondering what was going to happen next. When Mum still didn't come, I started to think that she'd never find us.

Rose was still clinging to me, her arms wrapped round my waist and I could feel her little body racked with sobs. I lifted her chin and saw tears pouring down her cheeks.

'It's all right,' I said, trying to sound cheerful. 'Mum'll be here soon.'

'But I've lost Goldilocks,' she said, gulping back her tears. 'Will Mum find her?'

The doll was precious to her, see. It was the one Dad had given her and she treasured it. But for now, I didn't know how she would ever get it back.

'Don't you worry,' I said. 'Mum won't be long.'

It suddenly crossed my mind that Tommy might not find Mum. What if she was waiting at the entrance or something? What if she couldn't see us standing here? I didn't like breaking my promise to Tommy, but I had to go and look.

'Come on,' I said to Rose. 'Let's go round the corner. Mum might be waiting for us there.'

I tugged her hand and hurried towards the entrance, my heart thumping against my ribs. By this time most of the people had gone from the front of the tube station – but Mum wasn't there. My heart dropped into my boots.

'Where is she?' wailed Rose. 'You said she'd be here.'

'She must be on her way,' I said and held her close while my eyes were suddenly fixed on the road in front of me and I saw what had caused the damage in the tube station. It was as clear as day cos the road was lit up with the flames from burning buildings. But I could hardly believe my eyes.

In Balham High Road, close to the entrance of the station, there was a hole. A massive great hole. A crater caused by a bomb. It was enormous. Gigantic. Huge. But what shocked me most of all was that, right in the middle of the hole, nose down, was a double-decker bus.

'Good grief!' I said. 'Look at that, Rose!'

She wiped the tears from her eyes and looked. 'Why's that bus in that hole?' she asked.

'I suppose the driver didn't see it in the blackout.'

I stared down the road. Some shops that had been there that morning were now just heaps of burning rubble. Woolworths, the biggest of them all, was gone. Houses had been hit, too, and I wondered how many people had lost their homes. People I knew. Some of them killed, probably. I couldn't take it in. I began to shake. My stomach churned and griped so much that I bent over and vomited onto the pavement.

I wiped my mouth with the back of my sleeve and looked up again. People were working hard to help. Members of the Red Cross were hurrying backwards and forward, bringing the injured out of the station on stretchers. I held Rose's hand and looked at every one that passed us in case it was Mum. But it never was.

Then a warden came over. 'You can't stand there,' he snapped. 'Haven't you got a grown-up with you?'

'Yes,' I said. 'We're waiting for our mum.'

Rose looked up at him and broke down in tears once again. 'Where is she?' she sobbed.

He probably felt sorry for us. Suddenly he wasn't so cross. He looked at me and said, 'Where is your mum, son?'

I pointed to the entrance. 'She's down there,' I said. 'We've been waiting for her but she didn't come. Tommy went to look for her.'

'Who's he then?'

'He's a friend. He's quite old and he's got a grey beard. But he's not come back.'

The warden turned round and beckoned to a tall lady in a dark green uniform who came hurrying over.

'Two customers for you, Mrs Bartley,' he said.

The lady in green smiled. She had a kind face and I knew she would help us if she could. 'Hello. I'm Mrs Bartley,' she said. 'Are you two lost?'

'No,' I said. 'We're waiting for our mum. She's down in the tube station helping Mrs Scott, but she hasn't come out yet.'

The lady looked at the warden and frowned. 'I think I'd better take these youngsters somewhere safe,' she said, and the warden nodded.

'We're not going without Mum,' I protested.

'No, we're not,' sobbed Rose. 'I want my mum.'

I took hold of her hand before I explained things to Mrs Bartley. 'We promised Tommy we'd wait just over there. You see, he's gone to fetch Mum and they won't know where we are if we go with you.'

The warden put his hand on my shoulder and moved us away as the ambulance men brought up another stretcher. 'What's your mum's name, son?' he said, pulling out a notebook.

'Mrs Ruby Wilson.'

'Address?'

'Thirty-four, Fernlea Road.'

'Right then, I shall be sure to tell your mum that you're safe and well when she comes out. And if I see Tommy, I'll tell him too. Now I want you to go with this lady. She'll find somewhere for you to stay till morning. Old Hitler's bombs are coming down thick and fast tonight. It ain't safe for you out here.'

As he spoke, another wave of Nazi planes passed overhead, black against the blazing sky. Then we heard the *crump, crump, crump*, as more bombs landed.

'Come on! Quickly now!' said Mrs Bartley, grasping our hands, and we ran with her through the streets of Balham, among all the noise and chaos. Though I'd lived there all my life, I didn't know where we were running to. I was too scared to worry about it.

'Here we are,' panted Mrs Bartley as she led us through the gates and into the playground of a school. 'There's an air-raid shelter over there.' She pointed to a low concrete building as we ran across. But when she pushed against the door, it hardly opened at all. 'It's full,' she said. 'Lots of people must have come from the underground. Come on, we'll go inside the school. There'll be space for us there.'

She was trying to stay calm, but I could see she was worried. Without pausing for breath, we raced back across the yard to the main building and in through a door marked 'Girls' and slammed it shut behind us, glad to keep out some of the noise.

A man in army uniform was standing in the corridor. Mrs Bartley rested her hand on the wall, gasping for breath. 'The air-raid shelter's full,' she panted. 'I need to get these children somewhere safe.'

'I know,' the man said. 'It's been a terrible night. Never had such bombing. Take 'em into the basement, will you? There's not much room, but they'll be safe there.'

We followed Mrs Bartley along a passageway and down some stone steps, which led to a small, square room lit by candles. In the corner was an old boiler, which didn't seem to be working, judging from the cold, but at least the room was dry.

There were people already in there sitting on blankets on the floor. There was a family – a mum, a grandad and three kids. There were four other kids, as well. They were by themselves and looking as scared as we felt – except for one boy with hair cut so short that he looked almost bald. He didn't look scared at all.

The grandad, who had bushy white eyebrows and a large nose, was very friendly. 'Come in, young 'uns,' he said. 'Are you on your own?'

I didn't know what to say so I didn't say anything.

'They've been separated from their mum,' said Mrs Bartley. 'I brought them here so they'd be safe from the bombing.'

Then she turned to us and handed us two thick grey blankets off a shelf. 'And here's a towel, too,' she said. 'Take your shoes and socks off and rub yourselves down. Then you can try to get some sleep. I'm sure everything will be as right as rain in the morning.'

'A-are you s-staying with us?' sobbed Rose who was shaking with fear, her little teeth rattling as she spoke.

Mrs Bartley's smile faded and she shook her head. 'I'm sorry, dear. I have to go. But these kind people will look after you.'

'Course we will,' said the grandad. 'Come over here, Tuppence.'

But Rose shook her head, grasped Mrs Bartley's hand and wouldn't let go. 'I want you to stay and look after us. *Please!*'

'I must go back,' said Mrs Bartley, trying to explain. 'I have to help some other children who might be in trouble.'

Tears ran down Rose's cheeks. 'I want Mum! Where is she? Billy said she'd come.'

Mrs Bartley took out a hankie. 'Don't cry, dear,' she said and wiped Rose's face. 'There, that's better. Now promise me you'll be a good brave girl.'

Rose looked at her with wide eyes. Then she sniffed and nodded and let go of her hand.

Once Mrs Bartley had gone, I dried the two of us with the towel as best I could. Then I lay down on the blankets with Rose clinging to me like a limpet.

'Mum will come and find us, won't she, Billy?' she asked.

'Course she will,' I said, 'She'll come running down them steps in the morning with her pink curlers in. You'll see.'

But inside I didn't feel as confident as I pretended to be. I had never felt more scared. My stomach was churning and I couldn't get the sight of them stretchers out of my mind. Some people had been badly injured down the tube station. I'd seen them carried out to the ambulance covered in blood and moaning. One man was dead. Even though I'd never seen anybody dead before, I was sure of it. He lay still as stone on the stretcher. Not breathing. Not moving at all.

But I was certain that Mum wasn't dead. She was somewhere helping Mrs Scott and the babies because that was what Mum was like. She was kind and always helping people. We'd see her tomorrow morning and she'd tell me I shouldn't have worried.

That's what I told myself, but as I lay there on that blanket I felt like crying. But boys from Balham didn't cry – even when their hearts were breaking.

Ten

Meeting Major Brown

I woke to someone shaking my shoulder.

'Up you get, son. It's morning. I expect you'll be wanting to go home.'

I suddenly remembered where I was and sat up with a start. The grandad was leaning over me.

'Is she here? Is my mum here yet?'

'I haven't seen her, son,' he said. 'But that don't mean she ain't looking for you.'

My heart sank.

'I think you'd better go back home now. She's probably waiting for you and wondering where you are.'

The other kids were waking up, too. Some were already standing and brushing coal dust off their clothes – the floor by the old boiler was covered with it.

My sister was still asleep. 'Come on, Rose,' I said, nudging her gently until she opened her eyes. 'It's morning. Let's go. We need to find mum and let Sheeba out of the shelter.'

Rose sat up and stared nervously at the grandad and his family as they walked out of the door, leaving me, Rose and the four other kids.

One of them was a boy about my age. I'd noticed him last night. He was skinny and very dirty with hair hacked close to his head.

'I'm going upstairs,' he said. 'There'll be some breakfast in the hall. It's good stuff if you're hungry.' He picked up one of the grey blankets, tucked it under his arm and marched through the door looking quite chipper.

The other three kids, who were younger, stood there looking scared, but when we turned to leave, they followed us.

At the top of the stone steps, I walked along the corridor with Rose and the young kids following behind. There were two men sitting at a table at the far end, blocking the way. They were both wearing khaki uniforms, but they looked too old to be in the army. They were talking to the grandad and his family.

'We're anxious to get back home, Major Brown,' said the grandad, speaking to the smaller man who had silver glasses perched on the end of his nose.

'Quite so. Quite so,' the major replied, shuffling some papers on the table.

Then the mother, looking rather nervy, stepped forward. 'We're hoping our house hasn't been hit. I'm ever so worried after that terrible raid. Do you have any news?'

Major Brown leaned over the table – which wasn't easy owing to his large belly. He ran his finger across a map spread out in front of him. 'I don't think you need worry,' he said, pushing his glasses up his nose and sounding very important.

'There's no damage on Laitwood Road as far as I can see. But if you have any problems, come back and report to me.'

The family looked relieved. They all said, 'Thank you very much, sir,' – even the smallest boy who was no more than three years old.

'If you want breakfast,' said the major, pointing over his shoulder, 'you'll find the Women's Voluntary Service in the hall.'

But they shook their heads. 'That's very kind of you,' said the mother, 'but we'd rather get home.'

Once they had gone, the boy with the short hair stepped up to the table.

Major Brown peered over his spectacles. 'I've seen you before, haven't I?' he asked.

The boy shrugged, but didn't answer.

The other man frowned at him. 'Is that yours, sonny?' he said, pointing to the blanket under his arm.

Again the boy shrugged.

The major glanced across, puffing out his cheeks. 'Well spotted, Sergeant. I believe it's the property of the War Department.' And he glared at the boy. 'Were you intending to steal it, lad?'

The boy looked at the blanket and seemed surprised to see it there – as if it had tucked itself under his arm of its own accord. Then he pulled it out and handed it over without a word.

Major Brown sighed and shook his head before reaching for a piece of paper, which he put in front of him. 'The government insists that we take particulars of all children without parents and relatives. That's what this form is for. Do you understand? Now give me your particulars, sonny.'

'Don't know nothin' about particulars,' said the boy. 'What's particulars when they're at home?'

'For a start,' the major said, picking up a pencil, 'I need to know your name.'

'I forgot. All them bombs have wiped my memory clean away, see. Can't remember a thing.'

Major Brown glanced up at the ceiling and sighed again before asking, 'Where do you live?'

'Don't know that neither, gov'nor.'

'No parents?'

'I might have and I might not. I wouldn't know.'

The major groaned and turned to the sergeant.

'Take the boy to the hall, Sergeant,' he said. 'Get the ladies to give him a good breakfast. Maybe food will bring his memory back and then we'll know what to do with him.'

The sergeant walked round the table and took hold of the boy by the elbow. As he was led away, the boy glanced back at me and winked.

Eleven

A plan for evacuation

I stepped up to the table and waited for Major Brown to finish writing his notes. That done, he looked up at me and said, 'I hope you haven't lost *your* memory, lad. One boy without a memory is quite enough for today. With all these rules and regulations there's a great deal to do, you know.' He reached for another piece of paper and held his pencil poised to write. 'Now, shall we start with your name?'

'Billy Wilson and this is my sister, Rose.'

'Address?' he asked, keeping his eyes fixed on the paper.

'Thirty-four, Fernlea Road.'

'Any family?'

'Dad's in the army. Mum got lost down the tube station last night. I expect she's at home by now.'

When the major heard this, he looked up and set his pencil on the table. 'She was down the Balham tube station, you say?'

'Yes. We was with her, but she went to help Mrs Scott. We got out as quick as we could, but Mum didn't come out, see. We waited for her then that lady brought us here.'

As I spoke, the sergeant came back into the room and sat down.

By then, Rose was looking very upset and she pressed against the table, staring at the major. 'Our mum's looking for us, but she doesn't know we're here,' she said as the tears spilled onto her cheeks. 'Please will you tell her so she can come and get us?'

'We're doing everything possible, little girl,' said Major Brown, picking up his pencil.

'I lost my doll, too,' Rose wailed. 'I don't know where Goldilocks is and she'll be frightened. Will you find her, mister? Please!' Then she burst out sobbing and I put my arm round her and pulled her close.

The major looked up at me and sighed. 'The explosion last night was very serious. She can't expect us to go looking for dolls, young man.'

'She's only six, mister,' I replied. 'She don't understand what's going on.'

The sergeant leaned forward. 'You'll have to be a brave, son, and explain it to her.'

'Quite,' said the major, tapping his pencil on the table. 'There were hundreds of people in the underground station last night. You were very lucky to get out. Many people didn't.'

There was a hard lump in my throat and I couldn't speak. I felt myself shaking and I had to hold onto the table for a second to stop myself falling over. Was he saying what I thought he was saying? That Mum was dead? I took a deep breath to steady myself. Course she wasn't dead! That was a terrible thing to say!

'You ain't looked for her, have you? So how do you know she didn't get out, mister?'

The sergeant shook his head and the major continued.

'There are a lot of people unaccounted for and,' he coughed nervously, 'a lot of people er... unidentified.'

I didn't want to listen to this any more. I couldn't take it all in and I didn't want to believe what he was saying. 'We want to go home,' I said, but my voice was reduced to a whisper. 'Please.'

Rose had slipped her hand into mine and was holding it tight. I didn't dare look at her in case she saw the fear in my eyes.

The major leaned back in his chair. He took off his glasses and began to polish them with his handkerchief. 'I'm afraid that's not possible, young man. You can't go home,' he said and coughed to clear his throat. 'The government has ordered that children who have no one to look after them must be evacuated to a safe part of the country.'

'But we've got Mum to look after us,' I told him. 'She'll have gone back home. You'll see! Just let us go.'

Major Brown squeezed his eyes shut. 'You live in Fernlea Road, you say?'

'Yes.'

He returned his glasses to his nose and looked at the map on the table. 'Ah, yes. I thought so,' he said, running his finger across it. 'Fernlea Road was bombed last night. Many houses were flattened. It's completely unsafe.' He leaned forward, wagging his finger. 'Do you understand why we have to evacuate you, young man?' He spoke to me as if I was deaf...or stupid...or both.

'But we've got our mum!' I yelled. 'She ain't dead! I know it! She'll be looking for us.'

'Now, now, boy. There's no need to get into a state. The fact is your mother was most probably killed in last night's bombing. I know that's an awful shock, but these are terrible times and we all have to be very brave.'

'No, she can't have been!' I yelled.

The major sighed. 'She didn't come out of the underground, did she? You didn't see her?'

'No.'

'Then in the absence of your mother we must send you to Wales where there are no bombs falling. This is for your own good. Do you understand?'

I thumped my fist hard on the table and yelled, 'No, we ain't going nowhere, mister! We're staying in Balham.'

The major leaped to his feet, his face scarlet with anger. 'Watch your manners, boy!' he shouted. 'I say you can't stay in Balham by yourself. It's too dangerous – and there's an end to it!'

Twelve

An offer of help

Major Brown had collapsed into his chair and was mopping his brow with his handkerchief when the sergeant leaned over confidentially.

'Can I suggest something?' he said.

'It's no good,' the major replied, shaking his head. 'The boy won't listen and I have strict instructions to evacuate orphans. These children have no one to look after them and—'

'Perhaps you could interview the other children, Major. I'll take these two to the hall and give them some breakfast. I expect they'll calm down after that. The other boy seems better for having some food.'

'Oh, very well, very well,' said the major, flapping his hand as if batting an annoying fly. 'Just take them away. This is turning out to be a very difficult morning.'

We were led into a corridor by the sergeant, who seemed quite kind, really. Not a bit like the major. 'Follow me,' he said. 'The ladies of the WVS will find you something to eat. I expect you're very hungry.'

He took us into a large room that was probably the school

hall. Oblong tables covered in white cloths had been placed in rows with stacks of bowls, cups and saucers arranged next to steaming vats and huge teapots. There was a queue of people waiting to be served and they moved slowly forwards their shoulders bowed, holding out bowls, which ladies in white aprons filled with porridge from the vats. Most of the people looked hungry and exhausted as if they hadn't slept for days and I wondered if their houses had been bombed.

The sergeant took us to the end of the queue and held out a bowl for Rose. 'Get yourself some breakfast, my dear,' he said, and she wiped the tears from her cheeks with the back of her hand.

As Rose took the bowl, she looked up at him with her big blue eyes. 'Are you going to look for my mum?' she asked. Although she wasn't crying, her voice was tight and full of fear.

The sergeant smiled and patted her head. 'Don't you worry, Rose. We've got people looking for her. Now I've got to go, but I'll be back in a few minutes – so you have a nice breakfast.'

This seemed to cheer her up and we shuffled along with the queue and held out our bowls for the porridge.

As we were heading across the room to find somewhere to sit, I spotted the boy with no hair over in the far corner.

'Look who's there!' I said to Rose, hoping to keep her mind off Mum. 'That boy was in the cellar with us last night. We'll go and sit with him, shall we?'

He was bent over his bowl spooning porridge into his mouth as if he hadn't eaten for a month. When we stopped at his table, he looked up and said, 'Who are you?'

'I'm Billy,' I said. 'And this is my sister, Rose.'

He lowered his spoon for a moment. 'You were in the basement last night, weren't you?' he said, and I nodded. 'I'm All-Off.'

Rose frowned. 'All-Off? That's a funny name.'

'On account of my hair,' he said, rubbing the stubble on his head with the palm of his hand. 'I cut it all off, see. That's the way I like it. So they call me All-Off!'

We sat down. All-Off carried on eating his porridge and by the time he had finished, the bowl was so clean that you'd never guess there had been anything in it.

'That's good stuff, that is,' he said, wiping his mouth with his sleeve. 'It's my second. You need to get two bowls if you can. I've learned that.'

'You been here before?' I asked.

'Loads of times. It's the best way to get your belly full.'

'Where do you live?'

'Here and there. As long as it's dry.' Then he smiled and said, 'Last week I found a grand old place. It was only half bombed and there was a smashing bed with blankets and everything. Very comfy. But I came here last night. Knew I'd get a good breakfast, see.'

'Ain't you got no mother?' Rose asked.

'Naw. Not since August. They tried to evacuate me to somewhere miles from here, but I got away.'

'The man back there – Major Brown,' I said, nodding towards the door, 'he wants to send us to Wales.'

All-Off leaned forward and lowered his voice. 'If you take my advice, you won't go. I hear some terrible tales about kids who get evacuated.'

'Are they sending you to Wales?' asked Rose.

'I ain't going nowhere,' he said, grinning. 'When I've helped myself to some toast I'll slip out of here before they come and get me. There's a door round the back so I'll go out that way. I like being free and living on my own, see.'

'We don't want to go away, do we, Billy?' said Rose. 'I want my mum.'

I shook my head. 'It's that major. He's forcing us to go. He says our mum's probably dead. But he doesn't know. No one's checked and he's just saying that to get rid of us.'

Rose dropped her spoon in her porridge and turned to me. 'She ain't dead, is she, Billy?'

'No, she's just lost,' I said. 'And we're staying in Balham till we find her.'

All-Off wagged his finger. 'Don't have anything to do with them officials. They'll tie a label on yer jacket and put you on a train and, before you know it, you'll be up a mountain in the middle of nowhere and it's freezing cold.'

'What do you think we should do?' I asked. 'The sergeant's coming back for us any minute.'

'They're the worst. Them in army uniform. Don't trust 'em, that's what I say.'

'Then who do we trust?'

'You don't trust nobody,' he said. 'If you don't want to be sent away, come with me. I'll see you're all right.'

It didn't sound like a good idea to me. I looked at All-Off. His clothes were dirty and worn and a bit too small for him. I shook my head. 'No, thanks,' I said.

He stood up. 'Please yourself. You stay if you like, but I'm off before that sergeant comes back.'

He hurried across the room and, as he passed the food table, he helped himself to two slices of toast before disappearing round the back.

I couldn't help wondering if I'd done the right thing. Should we stay or should we have gone with All-Off? I didn't know what was going to happen next.

Feeling like I did, I found the porridge hard to swallow and I pushed the bowl away. Rose was eating hers slowly, sniffing tears away between each mouthful. I just sat there trying to think what to do. The more I thought about the major, the angrier I got. I was certain that he wasn't going to help us. He wouldn't even listen to what we had to say. He just wanted to send us away so he could cross us off his list. We needed to get out of there and look for Mum ourselves.

I got to my feet. 'Come on, Rose. Let's try and catch up with All-Off.' At the time, this seemed to be the best plan. He might have been a bit scruffy, but All-Off looked like the sort of kid who would know what to do next.

Rose looked up at me, her eyes wide with surprise. I reached out to take her hand, but before I could pull her to her feet, the sergeant walked back into the room.

Thirteen

The lorry arrives

The sergeant walked over to our table and sat next to Rose. 'Good porridge, is it?' he asked.

Rose nodded, holding onto her dish. She began spooning the porridge into her mouth as if she was afraid he might take it away.

Then the sergeant looked across at me. 'Have you seen the lad with the short hair?' he asked. 'I brought him here earlier.'

I shrugged, not wanting to give anything away.

'We did see him, mister,' said Rose, scraping her bowl clean. 'He was sitting here, but he's gone now.'

'That's a shame,' said the sergeant. 'Now he'll miss the lorry. Major Brown says there's one arriving soon to take you all to the station.'

I folded my arms across my chest. 'We ain't going nowhere. You're trying to send us to Wales, ain't yer?'

'Look, Billy,' said the Sergeant, 'the bombing was really serious last night, and who knows how bad it will be tonight. We've got to get you away from here.'

'You're not listening!' I yelled. 'I told you we're going to go and look for our mum. We'll find her even if you can't.'

The sergeant shook his head. 'We don't know where your mum is, son. She didn't come out of the tube station and we haven't found her yet. So we have to look after you. Do you understand?'

'You think she's dead, don't you? But she ain't. I know she ain't.'

He sighed. 'I know how you feel, Billy.'

'No, you don't,' I bawled. 'You *think* you know what it's like to lose your mum and to have people boss you around. But you don't!'

He put his hand on my shoulder, but I shrugged it away.

'What if I promise to go and look for your mum?' he said. 'I'll ask around if you promise to go to Wales where it's safe. You can write to me. Send me your new address and I'll write back and tell you what I've found out. How about that?'

'We can find Mum by ourselves.'

The sergeant frowned and looked really worried. 'It's dangerous in Balham now. I want you and Rose to go somewhere safe. Your mum would want that, wouldn't she?'

Rose tugged at my sleeve. 'Why are you shouting, Billy? When can we go home?'

The sergeant crouched down on a level with Rose and smiled as sweet as you like. 'You're going to Wales, Rose. There'll be lots of sheep there.'

I knew what he was up to. He was trying to persuade Rose to go and then I'd have to go with her. All-Off was right. These officials just tell you what to do – whether you want to do it or not.

That's what I was thinking when Major Brown marched briskly into the hall followed by the other three children we'd met in the basement.

'What's the hold-up, Sergeant?' he said as he came over to our table. 'We've got to get moving. The lorry's arrived. Mustn't keep them waiting. I've written the labels for the children – names and addresses and everything – so, once we've tied them on their coats, we can send them on their way.'

'We ain't going,' I said, but straight away the major stepped over and gripped my arm.

'Now, now, sonny,' he said. 'We'll have none of that. It's all for your own good. There's a war on, you know.'

They tied labels on our coats like All-Off had said they would – as if we were pieces of luggage. And when they'd finished, they marched the five of us down the corridor and out into the school yard where a lorry was waiting. I hated that lorry as soon as I saw it. It was taking us away from home, away from Mum.

The driver jumped out of his cab and let down the wooden flap at the back. There was a group of kids – some about the same age as us – already sitting inside staring out at us with faces as miserable as ours.

'Right,' said the sergeant. 'In you get.' He was in charge of lifting us into the lorry. One by one he picked up the younger kids as if they were sacks of potatoes and put them on board.

Rose's face turned ashen when he lifted her in, but she didn't say a word. I don't think she knew what was going on. When it was my turn, I didn't go easy.

'I'm not going!' I yelled, and I thrashed about, trying to get free. But that sergeant was strong and he lifted me inside, still struggling, so that I crashed onto the floor. 'You can't do this. You're kidnapping us. How will my mum find us? She'll be worried sick.'

I scrambled to my feet as the sergeant lifted the wooden flap at the back of the lorry and replaced the metal pins that held it in place. I sat on a wooden bench holding my head in my hands and Rose sat next to me. She tried to put her arm round me but I brushed her off and turned away, frightened that I might blub – and I didn't want anyone to see that – 'specially not in Balham.

The driver started up the engine and the lorry set off down the road. I turned to Rose and saw that she was crying again. She wasn't making a noise or anything, but tears were trickling down her face and dripping off the end of her chin. It was my fault. I'd made her cry. I'd pushed her away because I felt bad that I couldn't sort out the mess we were in.

'We'll be all right, Rose,' I said, reaching out for her hand. 'Don't you worry. I'll think of something.'

She sniffed and wiped her cheeks. 'But Mum's gone and now we won't ever see Sheeba again.'

Sheeba! I'd been so busy worrying about Mum, I'd forgotten about my dog. I'd left her in the shelter with no way of getting out. She had water – a big bowlful – but she would have run out of food.

As the lorry headed towards the centre of London, my head

was spinning. I knew I couldn't go to Wales. I wouldn't go. I had to get us back to Balham, and to Sheeba, as soon as possible.

Fourteen

A bumpy ride

At the back of the lorry a lady was sitting with some older kids. She was wearing a plum-coloured coat and a hat to match. Mum had a hat that colour. It was her favourite. Dad used to say she looked like the Queen in it.

'Who's that lady?' whispered Rose, who had stopping crying by then.

'She don't look like one of them officials,' I replied. 'She might be a teacher.'

'Is she kind, Billy?'

I shrugged. 'I don't know. We'll have to see.'

Once we were on our way, the lady came down to talk to us and asked our names. She was nice enough, I suppose. She was only trying to be friendly, but I didn't want to talk.

'I'm afraid it's a bit of a bumpy ride,' she said, smiling and showing off a row of big teeth that reminded me of our milkman's horse, Buttercup. 'It won't be long before we arrive at Paddington Station then you'll be able to get on the train. That will be exciting, won't it?'

Some of the other kids thought this was a real treat. I bet

they'd never been on a train before. Not like me. I'd been up to Yorkshire a few times, so it wasn't new to me. They were all talking about trains, but I just sat there desperate to get away.

The lorry was covered in canvas with an opening at the back that I could look through. We lurched along the bomb-damaged roads, juddering over rubble and swerving around ruts. I felt every bump, every pothole – and there were plenty of those. I kept my eyes fixed on the road, trying to remember the way we were travelling and the buildings we passed. If I managed to escape, I needed to know how to get back to Balham. I didn't want to ask directions in case people got suspicious.

We'd been on the way for three or four miles when the driver turned off the main road and, after that, I couldn't recognise any of the roads or buildings and I thought I'd never be able to find my way home.

The rocking of the lorry had sent Rose to sleep, but I sat there staring out through the gap, thinking of ways to get off. If I jumped out I'd probably break my legs and land up in hospital. What would be the good of that? And what about Rose? I felt helpless. A failure. Until suddenly, through the gap in the canvas, I saw Battersea Park.

'Look, Rose!' I said, nudging her awake. 'We went there with Mum and Dad. Remember?'

I thought it would make her smile, but her face crumpled into misery and she buried her face in my jacket as she remembered that day out. It had been warm and sunny and we'd had a picnic sitting on the grass. Egg sandwiches, currant cake and a flask of tea. Mum and Dad. Rose and me. Before the war.

When the park finally disappeared from view, the lorry rumbled on over a long bridge.

'Which bridge is this, miss?' I asked the lady, thinking that this information might be useful.

'Albert Bridge, dear,' she said. 'You can see the River Thames now.' And she pointed at the water down below.

Once we'd crossed the bridge, there was more and more bomb damage. Worse than anything we'd had in Balham. Big buildings: offices, banks, shops – all with their fronts blown off. The lorry driver must have had a hard time getting through, but he didn't stop. Sometimes he turned down side streets to avoid bomb craters and piles of rubble in the road. Somehow he kept going.

The lady tried to take our minds off the bomb damage. 'Look over there,' she said. 'There's Hyde Park.'

'Can we go and play?' asked one of the little kids. 'Are there any swings?'

She smiled and shook her head. 'We won't be stopping, I'm afraid. We'll be at the station in no time. Not far now.'

We were getting close to Paddington, but I still had no idea how we could escape from the lorry. The nearer we got, the more anxious I became. My cheeks were burning and I could feel beads of sweat breaking out on my forehead. My heart was racing so fast that I couldn't think clearly.

Then the lady announced, 'Five more minutes, children, and we'll be at the station.'

No! I thought. *I'm not getting on a train. If I do, I'll never get home. I'll never find Mum, and Sheeba will be left in the shelter to starve. No! No! No!*

Then, quite suddenly, my luck changed. One of them miracles happened. The lorry turned into another road, slowed down and, for the first time, it stopped. I stuck my head out through the opening in the canvas but of course I couldn't see anything at the front of the lorry. Then I heard the driver shout, 'What's going on, lads? I've got a lorry-load of kids and I'm trying to get 'em to Paddington.'

'Can't you see it's a bomb crater?' a man replied. 'You can't get down this street, mate.'

The lady in the plum-coloured coat came and stood next to me. 'I'll go and see what's happening,' she said as she pulled out the metal pins that held the wooden flap in place and let it down. 'I won't be long.' Then she sat on the edge and held onto her hat as she jumped down.

Most of the kids were hanging out of the back of the lorry trying to see what was going on. All eyes were on the lady – except mine. I was staring down at the road. The lorry was standing still. The flap was down. It would be easy to get away.

'Rose!' I whispered, and took hold of her hand. 'I'm going to jump off.'

'No, Billy, you can't,' she said out loud.

Several kids heard her and they turned to look at me.

'What are you doing?' called a boy with a runny nose. 'You'd better not go or I'll tell.'

I didn't care. I jumped off the back of the lorry, held out my arms to Rose and lifted her down.

'Now run!' I said.

We raced down the road and I was hoping none of the adults would see us. Most of the kids cheered, but one of 'em (I think it was the boy with the runny nose) shouted, 'Miss, miss! That lad and his sister's gone. Miss, miss!'

I held Rose's hand tight and we kept going to the end of the road. Then we stopped. Which way should we turn? Left or right? I didn't know. I wasn't sure.

'This way, Rose. Down here,' I said, tugging her hand and hoping I'd made the right choice.

Rose was panting by then. 'Are we going home to Mum?' she asked.

'We are,' I said. 'We're going back to Balham.'

I glanced over my shoulder. Nobody was following. Good! But just in case they were, I turned down one side street and then another so that if anyone came after us, they'd find it difficult to know which way we'd gone.

We kept running for a few minutes, dodging people on the pavement, pushing through crowds until Rose said, 'My legs hurt, Billy.' So I slowed to a steady walk.

By then I was confident that nobody was chasing after us. But I hadn't a clue which way we were heading.

I wondered if I should ask somebody how to get to Balham. But they might think it odd – a twelve-year-old boy and a little girl lost in the middle of London. I remembered what All-Off had said. 'Don't trust nobody.' He was right. They might take us to a police station or something.

I thought for a minute and remembered that the lorry had gone past Hyde Park. Maybe if I asked someone the way to the park it wouldn't seem so suspicious.

That was the plan.

The street was busy. People were walking fast as if they had important things to do, places to go.

'Excuse me, mister,' I called out to a smart-looking gent. But he didn't stop. He was obviously in a hurry.

'Excuse me!' I called to another man who didn't seem to hear me and kept on walking, his eyes fixed on the street ahead.

Then I saw a lady stop nearby and search in her handbag for something. I noticed she had creases at the sides of her eyes, which was a sure sign that she smiled a lot. So I decided to ask her.

'Excuse me, missus,' I called out and she looked up.

'Yes?' she said and she smiled a lovely big smile. See! I was right.

'Can you tell us how to get to Hyde Park, please?' I asked in my most polite voice.

'It's a very big park, which part do you want?' she said and looked down at Rose. 'Are you going to feed the ducks?'

'I don't know,' said Rose, who was having a very puzzling day.

'Yes, we are,' I replied before Rose could say anything else. 'She likes ducks, don't you?' And the lady laughed.

'Well then keep walking that way,' she told us and pointed

91

down the road. 'Turn right in about a hundred yards. Keep straight on and you'll be there in ten minutes or so.'

We set off and, for the first time that day, I felt hopeful. We were on our way home.

Fifteen

Eels and mash

Once we'd found Hyde Park, Rose insisted on going to find the ducks.

'I like ducks,' she said. 'Can I see them, Billy? Can I?'

What harm would it do? I thought. So we walked over the grass down to the big lake in the middle called the Serpentine, and she ran backwards and forward along the edge of the water waving her arms and calling, 'Come here, ducky ducks!' Some of them came up on the shore, but when she ran after them they soon flapped away again out of her reach.

'We can't stay long,' I called. 'We'll have to go.'

'Five minutes,' she said. 'Please, Billy.'

She was having such a good time and, for a little while, I felt happy, too. So I sat on the grass and watched her until a cold wind picked up and with it came a fine, miserable drizzle.

'We've got to go, Rose,' I called as I got to my feet. 'It's raining and it's a long walk home.'

Rose ran back to me, smiling. 'Are we nearly home now, Billy?'

'We'll have to walk some more,' I said, 'then we'll be home.'

But it turned out that Balham was further than I thought.

By the time I'd found the Albert Bridge it was the middle of the afternoon. The sky was heavy with grey clouds and the drizzle had turned to driving rain. Soon we were soaked to our skin, our shoes squelched and rain dripped off our hair. We were freezing cold and our stomachs were complaining that we hadn't had anything to eat since the porridge early that morning.

'We won't be long now, Rose,' I lied, just to keeping her going.

But she was looking miserable and dragging her feet as if they were too heavy to lift. Nothing I said would cheer her up. 'I'm tired,' she wailed. 'I want to stop.'

I tugged her along the bridge, which was busy with traffic going to and from the city. People on the pavement were hurrying through the rain to get to the other side of the river, umbrellas pulled low over their heads.

Suddenly Rose snatched her hand out of mine, sank down onto the pavement and refused to budge. I tried to pull her to her feet but she only flopped back.

'Come on, Rose,' I said. 'Don't be silly. You can't sit in the middle of the bridge. You can have a rest when we get to the other side. I promise.'

But she wouldn't move. She just sat there, sobbing, and people had to step round her to get past – which was very embarrassing as I had to keep saying, 'Sorry, mister' and 'Sorry, missus' over and over. She stayed sitting there making a terrible noise until a large man in a black coat and bowler hat came hurrying along holding his umbrella low against the driving rain. He didn't see Rose. It must have been quite a shock for him when he tripped over her and tumbled head over heels, landing on the pavement with a *whack!* His hat fell off then his umbrella blew away, so I chased after them while he sat rubbing his head, looking very puzzled.

'Sorry, mister,' I said when I returned, panting, to give him back the hat and umbrella. 'My sister's really tired. She didn't mean to get in your way.'

The man put the hat on his head and scrambled to his feet. 'My fault, sonny,' he said, rubbing his back. 'I wasn't looking where I was going.' Then he glanced down at Rose who was still crying. 'She looks very upset.'

Suddenly Rose stopped howling and looked up at him. 'I ain't upset,' she said. 'My legs is tired and my belly's empty!'

'Oh dear,' he replied and looked over at me. To my surprise, he dipped his hand into his pocket and pulled out a sixpence. 'That's a reward for retrieving my hat and brolly, young man. Get something to eat for you and your sister. There's an eel and pie shop over there,' he said, pointing to the end of the bridge. 'They'll have something.'

That was the best thing that happened that day. Sixpence to spend! I couldn't believe it.

'Thanks, mister. Thanks very much,' I said, but he just raised his umbrella and went on his way.

We were starving hungry and hurried to the pie shop and pushed open the door. As I stepped inside the smell of cooking almost bowled me over. It was such a delicious smell I stood there with my eyes closed, breathing it in and savouring it.

'You want somethin' to eat, son?' I opened my eyes to see a man in a large white apron standing behind the counter.

'We want a pie,' said Rose. 'We're very hungry.'

The man shook his head. 'No pies today,' he said. 'But you can have stewed eels. How's that?'

Rose looked at me and I nodded as I put the money on the counter, hoping that sixpence would be enough.

'You want mash with that, son?' the man asked.

Mash as well! What a treat! 'Yes, please,' I said.

'Yes, please,' said Rose. 'Mum makes mash. I like it.'

The man pointed to a table covered with a shiny brown cloth. 'You sit down,' he said. 'I'll bring it over to you.'

My mouth began to water at the thought of food as we walked over and sat at the table. It wasn't long before our wet coats began steaming in the warmth of the shop, which was very clean with walls covered in white tiles.

'Want a cuppa with these?' the man asked when he brought two plates of eels and mash and put them in front of us. 'You look as though you could do with one.'

I didn't say anything because I didn't have money for tea – but he brought it anyway. I think he must have guessed how cold we were.

The stewed eels were delicious and so was the mashed potato with special green gravy. By the time we'd eaten it all and drunk our tea, my toes were beginning to tingle and Rose's cheeks were flushed pink. We were so comfy, we could have stayed there all day, but we were a long way from home. We had to get back to Balham before it got dark and the air-raid siren sounded.

Sixteen

Clapham Common

By the time we'd left the shop, the rain had stopped and the sun had come out – a lovely red ball of fire hanging low in the sky – so I knew it was getting late. I remembered from Mr Patrick's geography lessons that the sun sets in the west and so I worked out which way was south. Balham was south of the river, south of Battersea Park. All I had to do was keep going in that direction until I saw somewhere I recognised – a road, a school, a shop. Anything.

We hadn't gone a mile when Rose started moaning again. 'My legs is hurting, Billy.' Then, 'My shoes is squashing my toes.' And, 'Why do you walk so fast?'

In the end, I picked her up and gave her a piggyback.

'How's that?'

'That's better. I can see a long way up here.'

Carrying Rose slowed us down and I worried that the light was fading. But I kept walking until the road came to a T-junction. The name on the wall was Clapham Common Long Road.

'Rose!' I said. 'Guess where we are! It's Clapham Common.

Do you remember it? It's not far from Balham. We'll be home before dark if we hurry.'

That put a spring in my step, I can tell you – even with Rose on my back. Being in the middle of London had been scary – not knowing if I was heading in the right direction, feeling lost. I'd never felt like that before. But now I knew we weren't too far from Balham, it felt fantastic. Like birthday and Christmas rolled into one.

On Clapham Common there were four big anti-aircraft guns with a group of soldiers standing by each one. They'd been there for months, ready to fire on any German planes that tried to bomb us. They were like the ones on Tooting Bec Common near to our house. I knew the noise – *rat-atat rat-atat*. I'd heard it often enough when we were in the Anderson shelter.

'Do you think you can walk now?' I asked Rose cos, by then, my shoulders were aching something shocking. She said she didn't mind, so I slipped her off my back and set her down on the grass. 'We can take a short cut across the common. It's the quickest way home.'

She grinned at me and nodded. 'I can run!' she squealed. 'Chase me, Billy!' And off she raced, surprising me with her energy. Suddenly all she wanted to do was play. But there was no time. The sun had almost disappeared and the light was fading. I didn't want to cross the common in the dark.

'No time to play, Rose!' I shouted. 'Come back. I don't want to lose you.'

But she went on running.

'Come back,' I called again.

Then someone yelled, 'Hey! You, lad!' and I turned to see one of the soldiers heading towards me.

'What are you doing on the common?' he said. 'You should be home by now. The air-raid warning will be going off any minute.'

I opened my mouth to speak, but he didn't give me time.

'Go on! Get yourself home. There's a war on, you know!' Then he hurried away in the direction of the guns.

When I turned back to look for Rose, I couldn't see her. I stared hard into the gloomy distance, but there was nothing. So I cupped my hands around my mouth and shouted, 'ROSE!' and listened for a reply, but there only the sound of traffic on the road.

Not knowing what else to do, I started running across the grass in the direction she had gone, calling her name over and over. When I came to a clump of trees, I stopped and then I heard something. It was Rose's voice. 'Billy! I'm here, Billy.'

Typical! Rose was playing hide-and-seek. How could she do that at a time like this! There was nothing for it but to go and find her. I pushed aside the low branches and went into the copse. The trees grew close together, and although I held out my hands in front of me, branches whipped against my face. It was a scary place. Very dark. I felt jittery.

'Where are you Rose?' I called. 'Stop messing about.'

Then I heard her voice again, but now she sounded very frightened.

'H-here,' she called. 'Come and find me, Billy. Please come.'

Jittery or not, I had to help her, didn't I? I was her big

brother. But the only way to reach Rose was to follow her voice. So I kept shouting and listening for her reply. It was hard struggling through brambles and stumbling over tree roots. More than once I fell. But at last, I found her. I almost tripped over her lying on the ground among some bushes.

'Rose!' I said, kneeling by her side. 'Why did you go off like that? Are you all right? What have you done?'

She started to sob.

I held her hand. 'Come on, now, get up and I'll take you home.'

But the sobbing turned into terrible wailing. 'I caaaaaan't. I've hurt my foot. I fell.'

I reached out in the darkness and felt for her foot.

'Where's your shoe?'

'My shoes hurt my toes so I took them off.'

As I lifted her foot I felt a covering of thick, sticky blood and she cried out in pain.

'You shouldn't have taken your shoes off, Rose,' I snapped. 'There's loads of shrapnel around here. Now you've cut your foot.'

I shouldn't have been angry with her, but I couldn't help it. I was worried. Shrapnel wounds could be bad. And now I'd have to carry her and it would take longer than ever to get home.

I bent down and lifted her onto my back.

'My shoes, Billy,' she sobbed. 'Find my shoes.'

'Where are they?'

'I don't know.'

I swore under my breath. Finding her shoes in the dark would be like looking for a needle in a haystack.

'There's no time. You'll have to leave them. We've got to get home.'

But she cried and sobbed and said she had to have her shoes. Had to!

'Well you can't,' I said. 'You should never have taken them off. We'll come back and find them tomorrow. You want to go and see Sheeba, don't you?'

At the mention of Sheeba, she forgot about her shoes, thank goodness. But pushing our way through the trees and brambles took time and when we got out of the copse, the light had gone completely and I couldn't see a thing. I felt sick with fear not knowing which way to turn. I stood there staring into the blackness until a breeze sprang up and parted the clouds leaving a space for the moon to shine through. It was a pale moon, but it was enough to light my way to Balham.

My back ached with the weight of my sister, but I managed to cross the common and at last I reached the road that would lead us home. It was the final stretch. But then the clouds closed over the moon and the air-raid siren sounded.

Seventeen

A safe cellar

The noise filled the air like a ghost wailing a terrible warning. Telling us to go and hide. Go now! Go quickly! Danger! Danger!

As I carried Rose piggyback, she clung round my neck tighter than ever, terrified by the siren. I hated it too! I wanted to clap my hands over my ears to block it out, but how could I when I was carrying my sister?

I staggered on along the road in the dark not knowing where to go for a shelter from the bombs that might fall at any minute, growing more and more frantic. It was dangerous to be out in an air raid. I had to find somewhere safe.

Then I heard a different noise. It was the hum of planes. Or was it a buzzing in my ears? I couldn't tell. My head was muddled. I wasn't thinking straight. I wanted to yell, 'Mum, come and help us!' But Mum wasn't there and I'd never felt so alone.

Then in the road ahead of us, I suddenly saw something coming towards us out of the gloom. Or was that my imagination? I stopped for a second to catch my breath just as the moon broke out from the clouds again and now I could see.

'It's somebody on a bike!' I said to Rose. 'What are they doing out here?'

Whoever it was, he was heading full speed towards us yelling, 'Oi! Get out of the way.' But I didn't move fast enough and there was the squeal of brakes as the rider stopped no more than two feet in front of me.

'Well, look who it is,' he said. 'Blimey! What you doin' here, Billy? I thought you was going to Wales.'

It was All-Off.

'We're trying to get back to home,' I explained. 'But Rose has hurt her foot.'

'You won't get there,' said All-Off. 'Listen to them Jerry planes. They'll be dropping bombs any minute. Come on. Sit Rose on the bike and come to my place. It's just round the corner and it's got a cellar. You'll be OK there.'

I'd never been so glad to see anyone in my life. Was this how Dad felt at Dunkirk when that boat came rowing towards him? I wondered. Now I felt the same. All-Off was like a miracle to me.

In no time at all, Rose was on the saddle behind All-Off, her arms wrapped round his waist, clinging on while he pedalled down a side street. I ran after them as fast as I could, but it was hard to keep up. I just hoped that the clouds wouldn't block out the moon again and leave me lost in the dark not knowing where to go.

All-Off suddenly stopped outside a large house – or what remained of it.

'This is it,' he called back to me as he climbed off his bike.

By the time I'd run the last few yards to catch up with him, I was gasping for breath. I wanted to stop, but there was no time.

'You carry your sister, Billy. I'll take me bike inside. Don't want nobody pinching it.'

As I wrapped my arms round Rose, the noise of German planes grew louder. I could hear the thrum of their engines and feel the vibration in the air. My stomach turned over.

'Look sharp!' All-Off shouted as he disappeared into the wreckage and I followed him inside.

He had a torch, which he shone ahead and I followed him, threading my way through the ruins of what had once been a large house – much bigger and grander than ours. But only three walls and half a ceiling were left. The rest was broken bricks and timber lying in a great heap on the floor. All-Off lifted his bike and scrambled over it like a mountain goat. But it was impossible for me.

'I can't get over,' I shouted to All-Off. 'Not carrying Rose, anyway.'

'Wait there,' he said. 'I'll put me bike away safe then I'll come and help you.'

All-Off climbed back over the rubble with the torch between his teeth and held out his arms. I passed Rose to him before climbing up myself and taking hold of her again. Rose didn't say a word or cry or yell. Too scared, I think. She just clung to me, trembling like a frightened puppy.

'That's the worst part of the house,' said All-Off once we were on the other side of the heap. 'This bit back here's not bad.' He shone his torch round the room that must once have been the kitchen and it was sad to see ordinary things smashed to pieces: chairs, cups and a teapot, a picture of a little girl. All broken. Ruined.

'I'll show you more later. Come on. We'd better get down to the cellar.' He went over to a door under what was left of the stairs.

'I'll go first,' he said as he opened it and went through. 'Watch how you go, mate.'

I followed him and saw a flight of stone steps, steep and narrow. But before I started to walk down, I was aware of a horrible smell rising up from the cellar. It was so bad that it made me want to throw up.

'Get a move on!' called All-Off as he shone his torch on the steps. 'Just take it slow. Come on. You'll be as safe as houses.'

My arms were aching with the weight of my sister and my stomach churned from the overpowering smell. I stood at the top of the steps, not wanting to go down to the cellar, but I knew I had to. I could hear the drone of the planes overhead. Bombs might drop at any minute.

I leaned against the wall to steady myself before I pushed my foot out and felt for the first step. I was so scared of falling or dropping Rose that I took each step very slowly and it was ages before I reached the bottom. When I did, I wasn't worried about the stink, I was so relieved to have my feet on solid ground.

'You did good, mate,' said All-Off. 'Sit your sister on the chair. I'll light a few candles.' He started fiddling with a box on the floor. 'Got to save the batteries, see? It was a bit of luck finding this torch. But if the batteries run out I don't know when I'll get new ones.'

The cellar was a surprise. There was no sign of bomb damage and the floor had been swept clean. In the corner there was a kitchen chair with a green satin cushion and against the far wall was a plank of wood resting on two towers of bricks. All-Off was using it as a shelf, stacked with tins, jugs, mugs and bits and pieces. There was a basin underneath and, best of all, there was a mattress on the floor, several blankets and a couple of towels. All-Off had certainly made himself at home! In the far corner was a heap of coal, and I thought that the poor family who used to live in this house would never use it now. I wondered what had happened to them.

While All-Off lit three candles, I carried Rose to the chair. She put her mouth to my ear and whispered, 'I don't like it here, Billy. It smells.'

I didn't say anything when I bent over to examine her foot. But Rose winced at the sight of dirt and blood.

'It'll be all right,' I said. 'I'm just going to wipe it, that's all.'

But she pulled her foot away from me at the thought of it.

'There's dirt in that cut, Rose. We don't want it to go septic, do we?'

I knew about cuts. Dad's brother hurt his leg playing football when he was a boy. Dad said the cut got badly infected and his brother died. I didn't want that to happen to Rose, did I?

All-Off poured water from a jug into an enamelled basin and brought it over. The cut was deep and when Rose soaked her foot she cried out as the blood oozed out and turned the

107

water pink. All-Off passed me a towel and, when I thought the cut was clean, I wrapped the towel round it.

'Thanks, All-Off,' I said. 'That should be on the mend by the morning. You'll feel loads better, Rose.'

'I need the lav, Billy,' she moaned.

'I've got one of them, too,' said All-off, pointing to the corner near the coal. 'See that bucket? That's the lav. Sorry about the smell. I didn't have time to empty it this morning.'

I wrinkled my nose. Now I understood what the terrible stink was.

We helped her over to the bucket and turned our backs until she'd finished, and then carried her back across the cellar.

'You can have the mattress, little 'un,' said All-Off. 'I dragged it down from the bedroom. It ain't half comfy. And there's blankets as well.'

We lowered her onto the mattress and she curled up, looking exhausted and miserable.

'You have a good sleep,' I said. 'And when you wake up in the morning, we'll be going home. I bet Mum'll be there waiting for us.' Then I covered her with a blanket.

'What about Sheeba?' she whispered. 'She's all alone in the shelter and she'll be frightened.'

I sat on the edge of the mattress and stroked her hair like Mum always did when Rose couldn't sleep. 'We'll let her out tomorrow,' I said. 'That will be all right, won't it?'

She was too tired to answer. Her lids fluttered closed and she fell asleep, despite the sound of bombs as they fell on Balham.

Eighteen

Waiting for the All Clear

Although the cellar was underground, we could still hear the droning of the planes and the noise of the bombs and it kept me and All-Off awake. So we sat on the floor wrapped in blankets, our backs against the wall, and talked.

'You didn't get sent to Wales then?' All-Off asked.

'Nearly,' I said. 'But we managed to get away before we got to the station.' Then I told him the whole story of how we jumped off the lorry and found our way back this far.

'You did well, mate,' he said. 'Now you're here you can stick with me and I'll see you're all right.'

I was grateful to All-Off for keeping us safe, but I didn't want to stay. Tomorrow I was going home.

All-Off told me about the house. 'It's quite a find, ain't it, Billy? Real grand. I found loads of things and brought 'em down here. Fancy some sardines, do yer?'

I wasn't in the mood. The smell from the bucket in the corner had turned my stomach and I wasn't hungry. 'No, thanks.'

'I've got a tin of Spam, if you'd like that?'

I shook my head.

In case he thought I was being difficult, I said, 'You've made this cellar real cosy, All-Off. So why did you go to the shelter last night?'

He looked at me. 'Why d'you think? *Hot food!*' Then he threw his head back and laughed. 'I ain't got hot food here so every so often I go and get a meal from the WVS ladies, see. I don't always go to the same shelter. I spread myself around a bit. Go to different ones so they don't get to know me.' He pulled the blanket up to his chin. 'If they think I ain't got a mum or dad, they try to send me away. You know – just like they did with you two. So I have to be on the lookout for officials like that Major Whatsit.' Then he gazed around at the things he'd carefully placed on the shelf. 'I'm comfy here, see.'

'But you can't stay here for ever, All-Off,' I said.

'Don't want to. If I find a better place I'll move on. Free spirit, that's me! I won't be bossed by nobody.'

When we talked about our families it turned out that All-Off's dad was in the navy.

'Last year, we had a telegram saying that he was missing. Mum said we'd got to keep our peckers up and he was sure to be alive somewhere.' He paused, leaned his head against the wall and puffed out his cheeks.

I didn't think he was going to speak again so I said, 'What are you going to do when the war ends?'

That seemed to cheer him up and he said, 'Well, my dad will probably come back and we'll find a nice house and we'll live together. But if he doesn't I'm going to be an explorer. See the world. I'll go to Australia. I've always wanted to trek across a desert and see kangaroos and that. You can come with me, if you like, Billy. Or are you scared you might meet up with them massive Australian spiders?'

I shook my head. 'It sounds exciting, All-Off, but I'm going to find Mum. No matter what that major said, I know she'll have got out of the tube station somehow. She's real clever.'

All-Off nodded. 'My mum was clever,' he said. 'She could turn her hand to anything: sewing, fixing things, growing carrots. Anything. When the war started she went and learned to drive a bus.'

'Wow!' I said. 'That's brilliant. I'd like to drive one of them when I'm grown up.'

All-Off grinned. 'Mum said we should all do war work. We should all fight for our country. And if she couldn't fight she said she'd drive a bus. Funny, ain't it? She went out in all weathers – and at night sometimes.'

Suddenly he went quiet and he pressed his lips tight. This tough-looking lad, with his cropped hair and grubby face, wasn't so tough underneath, I thought. I bet he missed his mum a lot.

He told me more after that – but his voice was so quiet it was almost a whisper.

'She was driving the bus in the blackout when a lorry crashed into her. It's hard to see where you're going in the blackout.' He gulped as if it was difficult to tell me the next bit. As if the words were too painful. 'That's how she died.'

I didn't say anything. I was remembering the bus in the crater outside Balham tube station. Remembering last night. Waiting for Mum by the entrance. Waiting and waiting. But she never came.

Neither of us spoke after that. We just sat there thinking our own thoughts until I heard All-Off sniff and I saw him wipe his face with his sleeve and I knew he was feeling bad.

He stood up and walked round the cellar blowing out the candles – all but one. When he'd done, he sat down again. He wrapped his blanket round his shoulders, leaned against the wall and closed his eyes. So did I. Somehow, in spite of the planes and the bombs and the big guns on the common, we must have fallen asleep.

We couldn't have been sleeping for long when we were both woken by a deafening, thunderclap-of-a-noise as a bomb exploded close by.

'Gordon Bennett! That was close!' said All-Off as the walls of the cellar shook, filling the air with dust from the mortar between the bricks. 'I hope me bike ain't damaged.'

'I'm glad *we* ain't damaged!' I said, getting to my feet. 'You can always get a new bike.'

'Says who? There's a war on, you know. Bikes ain't easy to come by.'

I went over to check on Rose. Despite all that noise, she was still sleeping soundly, but covered in grey dust. I quickly wiped her face with one of All-Off's towels and brushed what I could off the blanket without waking her.

'There ain't nothing we can do till the All-Clear sounds,' said

All-Off, rubbing his scalp to remove the dust. 'We'll see what the damage is in the morning. Let's get some kip, Billy. Can't do without sleep, can we?'

I wiped my face and spat the grit from my mouth. Then I sat down again, thinking about the bike Dad had given me for my birthday, wondering if it would still be in the shed when we got back home tomorrow.

Nineteen

Trapped

I was woken by the sound of the All Clear.

'Is it morning, Billy?' asked Rose as she sat up and looked around. 'Can we go home now?'

'Soon,' I said and I leaned over and nudged All-Off awake. 'What time do you think it is?'

'Dunno,' he replied, yawning and stretching his arms to get the stiffness out of them. Then he threw back his blanket and stood up. 'I'll go and see if it's light yet.'

The candle had burned low but he lit another before walking up the steps to the cellar door and turning the handle. But nothing happened. The door didn't open. When he turned it again and rattled it, still nothing happened. Then he tried pushing his shoulder against the door.

'It ain't moving, Billy,' he called down. 'It's stuck.'

I ran up the steps to help him and this time we both put our shoulders to the door and pushed. But it still didn't open.

All-Off stood there, hands on hips. 'It must have been that bomb last night. It's sent the door out of kilter – sort of crooked. Now it's jammed.'

I tried to think what Dad would do. 'Got any tools down here?' I asked. 'We could try and force it open with a screwdriver.'

All-Off scratched his head. 'There's a tin box under the bench. I think there's a hammer in it.'

I found the metal toolbox and opened it up. 'This should do the job,' I said. And I passed a screwdriver up to him.

All-Off pushed it between the door and the frame, but all that happened was that the wood, which was old and rotten, crumbled and left a small hole. The door didn't move.

I fetched a hammer out of the box. 'Let me have a go,' I said, sure that I could solve the problem. I hammered the screwdriver into the gap.

With all the shouting and the hammering, Rose wanted to know what was going on.

'The door's stuck,' I said. 'But I'm just going to prise it open. Won't be long.'

My attempt with the hammer and screwdriver failed. The wood just splintered again and broke away.

'Good try, mate,' said All-Off. 'But I think we'll have to smash the door down, if we're going to get out of here.'

He held out his hand to take the hammer and we took it in turns to strike the door before the wood finally split in the middle, leaving a hole the size of a dinner plate. Rose cheered. But it wasn't good news. When we looked through the hole, we could see that there was a huge pile of rubble heaped against the door. Although last night's bomb hadn't hit the house directly, it must have been near enough to send the bedroom floor crashing down.

'Don't worry, mate,' All-Off said, cheerfully. 'I'll make the hole bigger so I can get through.' And he raised the hammer again.

'No!' I said. 'That won't work.' But he took no notice and bashed away at the door – *bang, bang, bang,* until the hole was as big as a dustbin lid. Then he reached through and pushed some bricks out of the way.

He shouldn't have done that.

Moving a few bricks made the rest of the debris start to move. At first, small stones and broken pieces of plaster trickled through the hole and bounced down the steps. But I knew what was coming.

'Get out of the way, All-Off! Quick!'

I leaped down the steps as fast as I could. All-Off came after me, but not fast enough. The door gave way and rubble suddenly burst through like an avalanche – wood, bricks, plaster all cascaded down, knocking him to the bottom.

By the time the flow had stopped, he was lying on the floor, half covered in the debris. Not moving. The air was so thick with dust that it swirled around the cellar like a winter fog. I covered my mouth but it was too late. I'd already breathed it into my lungs and sucked it into my throat. I bent over, coughing and retching, my eyes running with tears while Rose screamed, before she began to choke, too.

Once the dust had settled, All-Off was so thickly covered that he looked like a stone statue. I kneeled down by his side and gently shook his arm. Then I leaned forward and spoke into his ear. 'All-Off!' I said. 'All-Off, can you hear me?' I was so afraid he was hurt – or dead. 'Can you hear me?' I repeated.

'Course I can hear you,' he said before he broke into a bout of coughing.

'He's all right,' I said, turning to Rose, and she smiled as she wiped dust from her face with her sleeve.

I started moving the rubble, piece by piece, from All-Off's legs. It was mainly plaster from the ceiling and some bricks. It could have been a lot worse. It could have been heavy concrete. But I had to move him as soon as possible. The steps were covered in debris and there was always a chance more would come rolling down.

When he'd stopped coughing, All-Off looked up and grinned. 'This is another fine mess you've gotten me into, Billy.' Which is what Laurel and Hardy say at the pictures, so it made me laugh.

I carried on tossing the stones and plaster into the corner and it was a relief when I'd cleared enough so that I could see his legs.

'Cheers, mate,' said All-Off. 'I'll be all right now.'

'Can you stand?'

'Course I can.'

I took his arm and tried to pull him up but he couldn't straighten his legs and he collapsed back onto the floor.

'Don't worry, All-Off. Leave it to me.'

I put my hands under his armpits and dragged him slowly across the floor towards the mattress.

117

'Rose,' I said, 'could you move over and make some space for All-Off on the mattress?'

'I can sit on the chair,' she said. 'All-Off's hurt. He can have the mattress and the blanket.'

'That's a good girl,' I said as she hobbled across to the chair with the green satin cushion and watched as I helped All-Off to lie down.

'Ta muchly, young Rose,' All-Off said. 'Good of you to give your bed to a poor injured soldier.' He winked at her and made her laugh.

His legs were cut and bruised, but I didn't think they were broken. He might have injured a muscle – maybe torn it – I thought. That's why he couldn't walk.

'My legs will be OK,' he said. 'But what about my bike? Supposing it's damaged?'

The bike was the least of my worries. With the door shut fast, I had no idea how we were going to get out.

Twenty

A heap of coal

'How are we going to get out now?' I asked.

All-Off lay on the mattress looking around the cellar before lifting his arm and pointing to a metal grille in the ceiling right over the pile of coal.

'Think you can get that off?' he said.

I stared up at it. I imagined the coal man would lift the grille off before tipping his sacks of coal down into the cellar. So if I could reach it and push it off, we could get out.

'I need something to stand on.'

'There's a couple of tea chests over there,' said All-Off. 'You climb on them, Billy. I bet you can do it. You've got legs like tree trunks.'

'I'll give it a go,' I said, laughing, and I went to fetch the boxes.

Before I attempted the climb, I cleared coal from the floor directly under the grille. Then I turned the boxes upside-down, lifted one on top of the other and stepped back to look at them.

'I'm not sure they'll be steady enough,' I said, shaking my head.

'Try 'em and see,' said All-Off. 'Go on. Climb up.'

Rose, who had been whistling 'London Bridge is Falling Down', stopped and said, 'Climb up, Billy. You're good at climbing. Go on.'

Rose was excited, but when I climbed onto the second box it wobbled so much that I didn't dare to stand up. Instead I crouched down, gripping onto the sides, thinking I was going to fall.

'I can't reach the opening,' I called down.

'You'll never reach it crouching like that, Billy,' said All-Off, resting on his elbows, trying to sit up. 'You look like a monkey squatting there. Go on! Stand up straight! You can do it!'

That was easier said than done. It was scary being so high up, but Rose was watching me and All-Off was cheering me on, so I had to give it a go.

As I tried to straighten my legs, they were shaking something awful. But slowly I managed to stand up so that my head was touching the grille. I felt like cheering – but I didn't dare. Instead I raised my arms, gripped the bars tight and tried to push. But the grille wouldn't move. I pushed again, harder, and it shifted a little. But at the same time I felt the chests wobble under my feet. If I fell from this height I'd be in serious trouble. I squeezed my eyes tight shut and held my breath, too scared to move, hoping the boxes would steady themselves before I gave another push.

When I'd calmed myself and felt my heart slow down to a steady beat, I opened my eyes and focused on the grille knowing that it was now or never. *Do it, Billy!* I said to myself.

Then I gritted my teeth and pushed on the grille as hard as I could.

It moved.

All-Off cheered. Rose cheered, too. But they were cheering too soon. I still needed one more push to make enough space to climb out.

I summoned up every ounce of my strength and with a low groan I gave one more shove. This time the grille slid away leaving the entrance to the chute wide open.

'I've done it!' I shouted and poked my head through the hole so that I could look outside and feel rain on my face. I gripped the sides of the coal hole ready to climb out, but when I did, the two chests wobbled and slipped from under my feet.

'Help!' I yelled as my legs dangled in mid-air.

'Help!' I yelled again – though I knew neither of them could help me. *What now?* If I let go, I'd fall.

'Pull yourself up, Billy,' shouted All-Off. 'Go on. You've got muscles like turnips. You can do it.'

He kept on shouting, 'Go on!' making me try again. Though I didn't think I could do it, somehow I heaved and pulled and I began to lift myself up until I managed to get my shoulders through the hole. My arms were screaming with the effort, but now my chest was through right up to my waist. Exhausted I flopped forward, my arms flat on the ground, and lay there panting. The air felt good, and once I'd recovered my breath, I dragged my legs up, too.

'I'm out!' I yelled. 'I'm really out!'

Twenty-One

Going home

A bomb must have landed in the road the night before. There was a crater not far from All-Off's house and more signs of bomb damage. But it didn't stop me from getting back inside and clearing away the rubble from the cellar door.

When I finally opened it, Rose's voice was the first thing I heard. 'Billy! Can we go home now?'

'Not long, Rose,' I called back. 'We'll be out soon.'

I climbed over the rubble on the cellar steps to find All-Off sitting up on the mattress. 'You done well, Billy,' he said.

'What about you?' I asked. 'Will you be able walk? Are your legs feeling OK?'

'Right as rain!' he said, trying to be his usual chirpy self.

I got on with clearing debris off the steps and when I'd finished All-Off said, 'That's great, Billy. Let's go! I reckon I'll be able to ride my bike and I'll take you home, Rose. You can sit on the saddle and I'll pedal. You'd like that, wouldn't you?'

'Yes, please,' she said. 'Can we go now, Billy? I want to see Sheeba.'

'Yes, we're going home,' I said for the hundredth time.

'Will Mum be home?'

'Maybe. We'll see.'

All-Off rested his hand on the wall and tried to pull himself to his feet. But he failed so I took his arm and helped him up the steps. It was hard for him and it must have hurt – but he did it.

Rose sat watching him. 'I can get up the steps by myself. You don't have to help me, Billy.'

'No, you can't,' I called down. 'Stay there, Rose. You've got a poorly foot and no shoes.'

Once All-Off was at the top, I went back and carried her up to the door, wriggling and squealing most of the way.

All-Off's bike was where he left it and miraculously still in one piece. He was desperate to ride it. But it was no good – his legs hurt too much. In the end, he sat on the saddle with Rose on his knee and I began to push them – very slowly.

The sky was heavy with the threat of more rain and the roads were covered with the wreckage of last night's bombing. Shops and houses had been damaged and the pavements and road were covered in rubble. It was a terrible sight and I wondered if anyone had been killed in the raid. People's homes were nothing more than heaps of bricks. Even buildings that were left standing didn't look safe. Some had great vertical cracks in their walls and, every so often, we saw gangs of men working to make houses safe where they could. They were too busy to notice three dirty kids.

It was hard pushing the bike, but once we were nearly

home, I felt a great sense of relief. It didn't last long, though. When I turned the corner into Fernlea Road, I saw that the Luftwaffe had done their worst. The first few houses looked all right, but some houses beyond ours were just ruins. The houses opposite ours had lost their front walls so that I could see inside where their best furniture was lying smashed among the debris. People in Fernlea Road took a pride in their houses and now some were wrecked and beyond repair. They had nothing left.

We were lucky that our house was still standing. So was Mrs Scott's next door – except for some broken windows and a crack that ran down the wall from her bedroom window.

'It could be worse,' said All-Off. 'Yours don't look so bad.'

'I suppose,' I said. 'Come on. Let's go inside and find Sheeba.'

I lifted Rose off the bike and carried her to the front door. I was surprised to see that it was hanging off its hinges. Just one push and it creaked open. I walked into the hall while All-Off hobbled slowly behind, bringing his bike inside.

'Mum? Mum, we're home!' I shouted, though I didn't believe she'd be there. Not really.

The hall was dark. I carried Rose towards the kitchen to keep her injured foot off the floor. As we got nearer, there was a strong smell of burning and when I pushed the kitchen door open, I couldn't believe what I saw. Brick rubble and dust were everywhere. The table and chairs were blackened and turned to charcoal. The stove had crashed onto its side. But worse, the whole of the back wall of the house was missing and left wide open to the garden.

I felt sick with the shock of it. It wasn't as if I didn't know about the Nazis and Hitler and bombs. It's just that I'd never expected our house to get hit. I'd thought it would always be there, waiting for us. Stupid, I suppose, but I couldn't stop a terrible feeling boiling up inside me thinking of that Jerry pilot flying his plane over our road and deliberately dropping his bombs on our house.

I stood in the kitchen, still holding Rose and shaking with anger as I stared out into the garden. That was a mess, too; a real chaotic jumble. There were bits of wood everywhere. Old Mr Wordsley's fence was down on one side and Mrs Scott's was down on the other, flopping over part of the veg patch. I was glad Mum couldn't see our house in such a state. She'd be really upset about the kitchen. I expect she'd have a cry, but once she'd wiped away her tears, she'd be absolutely furious.

I was thinking about this when I saw something move half way down the garden. Maybe it was a cat or a dog looking for food, I thought. But no, it was too big. There was nowhere to put Rose down but I managed to struggle over the debris into the garden to see who was there.

'Are we going to get Sheeba?' asked Rose. 'Are we, Billy?'

They must have heard Rose's voice cos three heads suddenly shot up from behind the broken fence. Three kids – filthy kids – leaped up from the veg patch and stared at me. Their hands were covered in mud and their faces weren't much better. The biggest one – about my age – had a sack over his shoulder and

I guessed from the bulge of it that they'd been digging up potatoes.

'Oi! What you doing?' I yelled.

As soon as they saw me they were off like scared rabbits through a hole at the far end. The big one went first and lost his cap as he pushed his way out. And the last one caught his shirt sleeve on a nail but he tugged at it and didn't seem to care if it ripped. One more hole in a scruffy shirt – what difference did it make? They were a right bunch of scallywags.

'You rotten thieves!' I bellowed as they disappeared. If I hadn't been carrying Rose, I'd have run after them and snatched that sack. Too late now.

Sheeba was making a terrible noise in the shelter. She'd heard our voices and was barking like mad.

'Oh, let's get Sheeba, Billy,' Rose squealed, struggling to get down. 'I want to let her out.'

'Careful, Rose! No! Keep still.' And I sat her on the edge of a broken wall.

I could see that the Anderson shelter hadn't been hit. I hurried down the garden, undid the catch and suddenly the door burst open and Sheeba erupted from the shelter like a rocket from a bottle. She leaped into the air, twisting and turning with yelps of joy. She was so glad to see me. Only when she'd finished her welcome, did she race up the garden to the farthest corner and squat down, leaving behind the most enormous puddle.

She came running back, saw Rose and went wild with delight and licked her neck while Rose hugged her and told her she was the best dog in the world and that we were very sorry she'd had to spend all that time alone in the shelter.

Then All-Off, appeared limping out of the house.

Sheeba turned and raced towards him barking fiercely. But I called, 'No, Sheeba!' and held up my finger. She stopped dead, her eyes fixed on the stranger.

'Good girl,' said All-Off, reaching out to pat her neck. 'I'm All-Off.' She sniffed his fingers then licked them as if she knew they could be best friends.

'Did you see them kids, All-Off?' I shouted as I went to take a look around the garden.

'Yeah, I saw 'em,' he called back.

I walked up to the veg patch. There were holes where they'd been digging.

'What a cheek!' I yelled. 'They've had some potatoes and a couple of cabbages – and maybe some onions.'

All-Off didn't seem bothered. 'I know them kids,' he said. 'I've seen 'em a few times up Tooting way. They're harmless.'

I stared at him. 'Harmless? They're thieves,' I said. 'Mum worked hard at that veg patch. And now some grubby little urchins have nicked most of the stuff. If I ever catch 'em I'll thrash 'em!'

All-Off leaned against the last remaining bit of kitchen wall and shook his head. 'No, you won't, Billy. They're hungry and they ain't got no home. But they probably want to stay round here where they belong. They don't want to get sent away.' He looked at me and grinned. 'Them kids are just like you and me, ain't they?'

I knew he was right. Hungry kids had to get food where they could. Maybe Mum wouldn't mind so much if she knew.

The shed where I kept my bike hadn't been damaged by the bombing. The outside lav and the coal house were still standing, too, but the doors had been blown off. In future, sitting on the lav wouldn't be private.

I thought I should go next door to see if Mrs Scott was at home.

'I won't be a tick,' I said and pushed my way over the collapsed fence.

I soon saw that Mrs Scott hadn't come home. To be honest, there wasn't much left to come home to. The back of her house had been blown away like ours, but it was in a worse state. The back bedroom floor had collapsed into the kitchen and one of the twins' cots was dangling from the broken floorboards.

I was sick at the sight of it and I felt sad, too. The last time I'd seen Mrs Scott was two nights ago in the underground, just before the bomb hit when Grace was poorly and Mum had gone to help her. Now another bomb had smashed her house. I couldn't help wondering where she was and if I'd ever see her again.

'Mrs Scott's not there,' I called as I climbed back into our garden.

'Do you think Mum's been back, Billy?' Rose asked hopefully.

'It doesn't look like it. But I'm sure she's somewhere safe,' I replied, trying to keep her calm.

Then rain began to fall and we hurried inside.

'I want to look at your foot, Rose,' I said, as I carried her through the wreck of the kitchen. 'Let's see if the front room's in a better state than this.'

The room at the front of the house was a mess, but nothing like the kitchen. Mum's little side table was broken and so were her china ornaments. But I found Dad's photo on the floor, wiped it clean and put it back on the mantelpiece. The settee, the armchair and the sideboard were OK – apart from a thick layer of gritty dust and a sprinkling of glass from a broken window pane. I sat Rose down on the settee.

'Yuck, it's dirty,' she said and I tried to brush the filth off with my hand.

Then I bent over to take a look at her foot, unwrapping the towel I'd put round it last night.

'I'm going to wash that cut again, Rose,' I said. 'Stay there while I get some water.'

The tap in the kitchen was still working. I filled an enamel bowl and took it into the front room along with a towel I'd found in a cupboard.

All-Off stood behind me looking down at Rose's foot. 'That's bad, that is,' he said. 'How you going to keep it clean, Billy? She ain't got no shoes.'

I dipped a towel in the water and began to wipe her foot. 'Wellies will be best, mate. They'll keep her foot dry and there'll be plenty of room for bandage,' I said. 'There's a pair in the hall. Will you fetch 'em, All-Off?'

He limped out of the room to find the boots while Rose

complained about my efforts at cleaning the cut.

'You're hurting me,' she wailed, screwing up her face and trying to push me away. The cut was deep and I kept wiping it until I'd cleaned away the dirt, but that only made it bleed again.

When All-Off came back with the wellies, he sucked his teeth at the sight of the blood. 'Crumbs!' he said. 'If I were you, Billy, I'd put some Vaseline on it. That's what my mum would do. Have you got any?'

'Yeah. Over there,' I said, pointing to the bottom cupboard in the sideboard. 'Mum keeps stuff like that in a tin box.'

All-Off found the box and, once I'd wiped the blood away and dried her foot, I smeared a layer of Vaseline over the cut and wrapped her foot in a strip of towel.

'You can put your wellies on, if you want, Rose, then you can walk about.'

She pulled her wellies on over the bandage and began to limp gingerly across the room. 'Look at me,' she said. 'I can walk now and it don't hurt much.' She seemed very pleased with herself.

'What about your legs?' I asked All-Off.

He shrugged. 'They're all right.'

But when I bent down to look, I saw several nasty grazes. His skin was torn and caked in blood and dirt and, although he made a bit of a fuss when I tried to clean him up, in the end he let me. I covered the grazes with Vaseline and wrapped a piece of towel round them, just like I'd done for Rose. All-Off smiled gratefully. 'Thanks, Billy.'

'When's Mum coming home?' asked Rose.

'I don't know,' I said. 'But I'm going down to the tube station to find out.'

All-Off raised his eyebrows. 'Shall I come with you?'

I shook my head. 'It'll be quicker if I go by myself.' Then I thought maybe I should put a clean shirt on. 'What do you think, All-Off?' I asked. 'Should I get some clothes from upstairs?'

All-Off looked me up and down. 'Naw! You look good enough to me.'

'Right,' I said. 'I'll be back as soon as I can.' I fetched my bike from the shed and set off to look for Mum.

Twenty-Two

The swimming baths

When I turned into Balham High Road, I saw how things had changed since the night when the bomb fell on the tube station. There was still a big black hole in the middle of the road, but the bus had been taken away and barriers put round the hole to stop people falling into it. Some policemen and Local Defence Volunteers were busy making things safe or clearing rubble. But there were no ambulances or fire engines. There were no sirens wailing and there were no crowds. Most of all, there was no panic.

I thought there must be someone who could help me find Mum. I was looking round, wondering who to ask when I spotted an ARP warden fixing a warning sign to a wall. *Danger. This building is unsafe.* He looked quite old – older than Dad anyway – with a grey moustache covering his top lip.

'Excuse me, mister,' I called, and he looked over to me, frowning. He was probably annoyed that I'd disturbed him in the middle of an important job.

'What is it, son?' he said. 'I've got work to do. I hope it's not a silly question.'

'It's not,' I replied. 'I was wondering if you were here when the bomb fell on the station.'

The man sighed as if he'd been asked this question a million times.

'No, I wasn't. I suppose you're wanting to know what it was like.'

'I know what it was like, mister,' I replied. 'I was down on the platform with my sister and my mum when the water came rushing through. Rose and me managed to get out, but Mum never came up, see. We don't know where she is.'

The man pushed his helmet to the back of his head. 'You're saying you lost your mum?'

I nodded. 'She was on the platform.'

'Oh dear,' he said rubbing his chin. 'That's hard, that is.'

'Do you know anybody who was there?' I asked.

'See him over there, son?' he said, pointing towards a tall policeman standing near the crater in the road. 'He might be able to help you. And good luck. I hope you find your mother.'

The policeman was checking something in his notebook, but he didn't seem to mind when I interrupted him. He listened when I told him what had happened, but then he said, 'Why haven't you got a grown-up with you, son? Is your dad away?'

'He's in the army.'

'Then who's looking after you?'

I remembered that All-Off had warned us about people looking for kids who were on their own. 'They'll send you off to Wales,' he'd said. 'You've got to be careful.' So I decided to lie.

'Our grandad's looking after us,' I said.

He looked puzzled. 'Then why didn't he come instead of sending you? This is no place for a boy.'

'I . . . er . . . Grandad's looking after my sister. She's ill, see. He sent me to talk to somebody. See what I could find out.'

The policeman nodded. 'Then you'd better get off home and tell your grandad to go down to the swimming baths.'

I looked at him blankly. 'The swimming baths? In Elmfield Road? Why? Grandad doesn't like swimming.'

The policeman looked embarrassed, then he cleared his throat before he explained. 'The baths are being used as an ARP depot now,' he said. 'But after that bomb fell on the underground, they had to find somewhere to take people.'

I looked at him blankly. 'Do you mean she might be there?'

His cheeks flushed. 'Er . . . yes. She might be, son. That's where they took all the people who'd died. There were a lot. Over fifty. They had to put 'em somewhere.'

My head spun and I closed my eyes, trying to block out the picture of Mum lying stiff and cold in an empty swimming pool with other dead bodies nearby. Maybe Mrs Scott and her babies, maybe Tommy, maybe total strangers. It was too horrible to think about.

The policeman put his hand on my shoulder. 'You tell your grandad to go to Elmfield Road and they'll have a list of the dead. Your mum might not be on it. In that case, she'll have been taken to hospital. Just tell him that.'

Now I understood. He was saying that if I went to the swimming baths, I could find out if Mum had been killed.

I didn't believe she had. But this was something I could do to be absolutely sure she was alive.

'Thanks, mister. I'll tell Grandad what you said.' Then I climbed onto my bike and set off in the direction of Elmfield Road, hoping that I wouldn't have to look at rows of dead bodies. The thought of it made me feel sick. But what else could I do? I had to go.

The swimming baths were in an old red-brick building. I'd been a few times with Dad when he was teaching me to swim. Now there were sandbags piled up outside the door and an ARP warden was standing on duty in his tin hat, smoking a cigarette.

'Excuse me, mister,' I said. 'I'm looking for my mum.'

The warden looked at me and winked. 'Lost her, have yer? Well, you've come to the wrong place, young 'un. I expect she's gone shopping – could be queuing up for something nice for your tea. I'd go to the butcher's, if I was you,' he said, pointing down the road. 'I bet she'll be there.' And he put his cigarette back into his mouth and took a long draw on it.

'You don't understand,' I said. 'We were all down the tube station when the bomb went off. But Mum didn't come out.'

His cheerful face suddenly clouded over. He flicked his ciggie onto the pavement and crushed it with his boot. 'That's different, matey. You should have said. Sorry, son. So she's missing, eh?'

'Yes. We don't know where she is.'

'Who's "we"?' he asked, narrowing his eyes.

'Me and my sister.' Without thinking I'd let the truth slip out.

'Ain't you got nobody else?'

'Our grandad,' I added quick as a flash. 'He sent me to ask about my mum. He said you'd know if she was here.' Another lie, but if it stopped us being evacuated it was worth it.

'Right,' he said, picking up a clipboard off the top sand bag. 'What's your mum's name?'

'Ruby Wilson.'

He looked at a piece of paper and ran his finger down a long list. 'Nobody by that name here,' he said. 'But that don't mean nothing. We ain't got names for everybody, see. What does she look like?'

'She's sort of medium height with curly blonde hair... Oh, but it might be straight if she got wet.'

'Right,' he said, turning to the door. 'You'd better come in and I'll have a word with Bernard. He's in charge.'

'Can I bring my bike in?' I asked. 'I don't want it to get pinched.'

He said I could so I lifted it inside and leaned it against the wall before following him down the corridor. Not that I wanted to be in a place like that. I was scared stiff, frightened of what I might see – but I needed to know about Mum.

As the warden pushed open a blue-painted door, a sickly stink drifted out so that I had to pinch my nose and cover my mouth.

'I don't have to go in there, do I, mister?' I asked. My legs were shaking and I had to hold onto the wall to steady myself.

'You stay in the corridor, matey,' he said. 'I won't be long.'

Once he'd gone through the door, I could I hear him talking

136

to another man – though I couldn't tell exactly what they said. I didn't want to know. And when he hadn't come back after five minutes or so, I was sure it was bad news. I closed my eyes and leaned against the wall, thinking I was going to faint.

When he finally returned his face was serious and he put his hand on my shoulder. 'We found a lady of medium height with blonde hair,' he said. 'But we can't be sure she's your mum.'

My heart lurched and seemed to drop into my stomach and my head began to spin. Was he asking me to identify her? No, please not that!

Then he said, 'Can you remember what she was wearing?'

I took a deep breath to calm myself down. 'She had a brown coat.' Then I remembered the earrings Dad had given her. 'She had gold earrings,' I added. 'They're like little hoops. She always wore 'em.'

The warden turned and went back through the blue door and I waited again. I imagined the two men bending over Mum. Pushing her hair away from her ears to check on the earrings. I dug my nails into the palm of my hand so hard that it broke the skin. But that pain was easier to bear than the pain of thinking Mum was dead.

When the warden returned he was smiling. 'Good news,' he said. 'That lady wasn't your mum. She was wearing a red coat and she didn't have any earrings.'

I felt sad for the lady in the red coat and I wondered if she had any children. But I was so happy to know that Mum wasn't there that I felt like singing!

Twenty-Three

The hospital

The sickness and dizziness I'd felt in the swimming baths soon went once I'd gone outside. I hopped on my bike and set off to the hospital like the policeman had told me to. Mum must have been injured. That made sense. Now I was going to find her and everything would be all right.

As I pushed off, I suddenly realised that I didn't know *which* hospital she'd been taken to. I turned back to the warden who was still leaning against the sand bags with a ciggie hanging out of his mouth.

'I forgot to ask,' I called. 'Where were the injured people taken after the tube station bomb? Which hospital?' Then I added. 'I need to tell Grandad.'

The warden raised his hand and grinned. 'Course you do! You tell him to go to St James on the other side of the railway line in Ouseley Road. That's where they took 'em. Good luck, son. I hope your mum's fine and dandy!'

'Thanks,' I said and set off, pedalling like mad and whistling 'It's a Long Way to Tipperary'. I was going to see Mum. All I had to do was ask somebody if I could speak to Mrs Ruby

Wilson. Easy peasy!

That's what I thought.

The hospital was an old Victorian building with a wide drive and a strip of grass in front of it. As I arrived, an ambulance drove in and disappeared round the back. I leaned my bike against a old oak tree before walking up some steps and in through a big mahogany door. Inside, there was a horrible smell that wasn't much better than the one in the swimming baths. I suppose it was disinfectant. Whatever it was, I didn't like it.

I found myself in a wide hallway. To the left of the door a lady in a smart grey suit, her hair pulled back off her face, was sitting at a large reception desk. People were waiting to speak to her but she was busy talking to a man and a woman and writing notes in a book.

Opposite the front door was a long corridor filled with lots of people in a great hurry. Nurses in blue uniforms with white caps. Doctors with stethoscopes round their necks. Patients in wheelchairs.

They were all too busy to take any notice of me as I stood there not knowing which way to go. Nobody asked what I wanted. Nobody asked why I was there, until a large, fierce-looking woman in a blue uniform came marching towards me. Her white cap was much bigger than any of the nurses' so I guessed she was very important.

'No children allowed,' she bellowed like the Queen of Hearts in *Alice in Wonderland*. I half expected her to say, 'Off with his head!' She stood glowering at me, her mouth turned down at the corners, her arms folded across her chest. 'What are you doing here, boy?'

'I'm looking for my mum,' I said.

'Why?' she asked – which I thought was a stupid question.

'The ARP warden told me to come. He thought she might have been brought here.'

This seemed to irritate her and her eyebrows slid together in a frown. 'A warden? Didn't he know that children aren't allowed inside the hospital?' She leaned forward as if she was going to bite off my head. 'Children are like mice. If they were allowed in, we would be overrun with them in no time. Then what would we do?'

'But there's only one of me,' I said. 'I won't overrun you, missus.'

She blushed pink. 'I am not "missus", I am Matron. And I expect a grown-up to come and make enquiries. You are not old enough to make enquiries, child.' She looked at me suspiciously and lowered her chin, which lay in folds around her neck. 'If your mother is in hospital, who is looking after you?'

That question again. It seemed that everyone wanted to know who we were living with. But I was ready with my answer.

'We live with our grandad, Matron,' I lied – again. 'He's looking after us.'

'Then I suggest you ask your grandfather to come to the hospital. It's disgraceful sending a child.'

'He's got bad legs, Matron. He can't walk. That's why he sent me.'

She puffed out her chest and grimaced. 'A boy of your age shouldn't be running around asking questions of medical people. You are too young,' she snapped. 'Now go home and ask an adult to come.' And she raised her hand and pointed to the exit.

I tried to explain, but it was no good. In the end, I turned away, my shoulders drooping with misery, and walked out. I'd failed to get any information about Mum and I wondered what I was going to tell Rose.

Outside in the fresh air, I began to feel angry. *Really angry*. Why was it that people never took children seriously? Why hadn't that matron let me explain? I could have told her about the bombing and how we'd lost Mum. But she wouldn't listen.

I hurried over to the tree to collect my bike and rode out of the gate, grinding my teeth as I pedalled home.

When I turned into Fernlea Road it seemed strangely quiet. It was now a wreck of what it had been. Some of the neighbours must have left – gone to find somewhere safe to live – and it felt like a foreign country.

I pushed our front door open and stepped into the hall. 'I'm back!' I shouted.

Sheeba came bounding towards me, her tail wagging furiously, glad that I was home again.

In the front room Rose was dozing on the settee.

'You've been a long time,' said All-Off. 'Any luck?'

I shook my head and told him everything I'd done – the tube station, the swimming baths and the hospital. 'It's been a waste of time, if you ask me,' I said, perching on the arm of the settee. 'They wouldn't even tell me if Mum was in the hospital.'

'Bad luck, pal,' said All-Off getting slowly to his feet. 'But don't let 'em beat you. We'll think of a way to find her.'

I didn't feel hopeful. 'I'm starving,' I said. 'My belly's griping. I haven't eaten since the pie shop yesterday. '

'I found a loaf in the bread bin,' he said. 'It's a bit stale but not mouldy. Rose and me had Spam sandwiches. They tasted good and we saved enough for you.'

I wondered how he'd been able to find anything in a kitchen filled with dirt and rubble – but I was too hungry to ask. I could see that he'd tidied the front room. He'd cleared the top of the sideboard, covered it with one of Mum's towels and put the bread and an open tin of Spam on top.

'I found a few things,' he said as he cut a slice of bread.

'So we're not going to starve then?' I said.

'Not likely!' he said. 'You've still got stuff growing in that veg patch. Them kids didn't take it all.'

All-Off placed a piece of Spam between two thick slices of bread and passed it to me.

'Thanks,' I said, opening my mouth as wide as I could to accommodate the sandwich. 'Smashing!' I said when I could speak again. 'The best sandwich I've ever tasted.' I suppose being ravenously hungry had something to do with it.

I finished the last bit and licked the crumbs off my fingers. 'There's some coal out in the coal shed,' I told him. 'Why don't we light a fire in the front room? Make it nice and cosy?'

All-Off sighed as if I'd said something stupid. 'If we light a fire, somebody will be sure to see the smoke coming out of the chimney,' he said. 'What if one of the neighbours comes round to find how you're managing since the bombing? What if they call in to see your mum?'

'But she's not here, is she?' I replied.

'Exactly,' said All-Off. 'And when your nosey neighbours find you're on your own, they'll stick a label on you and send you off to Wales before you can say "Winston Churchill".'

So we couldn't light a fire. Just one more thing to make living difficult. I slumped into the armchair and covered my eyes, trying to think what to do next. Trying to think how to find Mum. I couldn't go to the police for help. They'd say, *You need to be evacuated right away.* That's what they'd say. They wouldn't let us stay in Balham. They'd make us leave Mum behind.

No! No! No! I wouldn't!

I didn't want to go on living like this – but who could I ask for help?

Twenty-Four

All-Off's plan

I tried to put the worries about Mum to the back of my mind, thinking that I'd come up with an answer in the morning. And later on, Moaning Minnie gave me something else to worry about.

'Down to the shelter! Come on!' I said and went to fetch our gas masks.

Rose started to sob. 'No, please, Billy. I don't want to go. It's horrible in there.' I knew what she meant, but I promised Dad I'd look after everyone.

'Rose is right, Billy,' said All-Off. 'While you were away I went and looked in the shelter. It's more like a swimming pool now. Honest, your Dad wouldn't want you to go there.'

'Then where?' I said. 'We can't go down the tube station.'

'I think we'd be safe enough in that cupboard under the stairs,' he said. 'The stairs are solid and it's a good old cupboard, that is. Dry and warm. Couldn't be better. What do you think, Billy? Take some cushions and we'll be snug as a bug in a rug.'

All-Off had experience of finding safe places and I trusted him. He seemed to know what to do, so I agreed.

As the air-raid siren wailed on, we hurried to the cupboard taking cushions from the settee. There wasn't much room for the three of us and Sheeba – but we were comfy enough and we took a candle.

'I liked it under the stairs with Mum,' said Rose, remembering how we went there at the beginning of the war. 'We played games. Can we play now, Billy?'

We tried I Spy, but we couldn't see much in the cupboard so we started singing as loud as we could to block out the noise of the Nazi planes overhead and the ack-ack guns on the common. The raid went on for ages and when we got tired of singing, Rose wrapped her arms round Sheeba, snuggled up on a cushion, and fell asleep.

I sat there hugging my knees. 'How do I get to see Mum?' I said to All-Off. 'I bet she's really worried. She'll be wondering where we are and if we're all right.'

'Worrying don't do nobody no good,' he said. 'You've just got to bide your time. That's what my mum always said. Everything will work out OK in the end.'

I shook my head. 'I can't go on living in this mess.'

All-Off looked slightly offended. 'It ain't so bad.'

'Look at us!' I said. 'We're filthy. There's no soap. We can't have a proper wash and we haven't had a decent meal all day.'

He winked. 'Leave it to me, Billy. I'll see we're all right tomorrow.'

I sank my head into my hands. He didn't understand. I didn't want us to live like rats in the rubble. It was too dangerous. I wanted Rose to be safe. I wanted to find Mum and go to Yorkshire. Together.

I lifted my head and looked at All-Off. 'It's no good,' I said. 'Somehow I've got to get into that hospital and see if Mum's there.'

All-Off leaned back against the wall.

He went quiet for a long time, and I thought he'd gone to sleep. But he hadn't.

'I'm thinking,' he said. Then, sometime later, he opened his eyes and grinned at me.

'Are you up for a bit of an adventure? Like in the comics?'

I wasn't in the mood for that kind of thing so I shrugged and turned my head away.

'Come on, Billy. Don't you want to hear my idea?'

I looked across at his eager face. 'I suppose you're going to tell me, aren't you?'

All-Off nodded. 'Listen! Hospitals have got loads of windows. Right?'

I grunted.

'My thinking is that they're too busy to make sure that they're all locked up. I'm good at getting through windows, see.'

'So your brilliant idea is to climb through a window?' I sneered. 'Don't you think somebody might notice?'

All-Off's grin grew wider. 'Not if we go during the night, Billy boy.'

'What?' I couldn't believe he'd suggested such a stupid thing. 'Are you expecting us to run through the streets when the Jerry bombs are falling?'

'Calm down, mate, and listen. What we do is wait for the All Clear. If it comes before it gets light, then we'll go. We'll black our faces so we won't be spotted. I've seen it in the films.'

I groaned. So All-Off had seen it in a film! I might have known. 'You're mad, you are. It's a daft idea. I'm going to sleep.'

I lay down with my head on one of the cushions and tried to think of another way to find Mum. I must have fallen asleep because I was woken by the sound of the All Clear. I hadn't a clue what time it was but All-Off had opened the cupboard door and was out in the hall.

'It's still pitch-dark out there,' he said. 'Let's get over to the hospital. It's at least an hour before it gets light. Come on, Billy. Get moving.'

If I'd been thinking clearly, I'd have said no. But I was half asleep and no better plan had come to me during the night so I went along with him.

'We'll have to take Rose with us,' he said, 'but we'll leave Sheeba to guard the house. Don't want any kids slipping in and pinching stuff.'

'I thought we'd frightened 'em off.'

'There are plenty more kids around. There are loads like us living in bombed-out houses. Didn't you know?'

I scrambled to my feet and joined him in the hall. 'I thought most kids had been evacuated.'

147

'Some have. Some haven't.' He looked at me and grinned. 'I know plenty who look after themselves. They keep quiet, see. Come on, Billy. Get your bike. I'll wake Rose.'

Before we left, we covered our faces with soot from the fire. Rose thought it was a game and she had great fun spreading it from her forehead down to her neck – though she made a terrible mess of her jumper.

'Now nobody'll see us in the blackout,' All-Off explained, and I had to agree it was probably a good idea. We didn't want to be spotted by the police.

As we climbed onto our bikes and set off for the hospital, there was only one thing on my mind – finding Mum.

Twenty-Five

The night trip

Clouds covered the sky that night. No moon, no stars were visible and the sharp wind froze my knees. Riding a bike in the dark was tricky. I had to strain my eyes looking out for potholes or bomb damage in the road.

Rose was sitting on the saddle behind me clinging on while All-Off followed on his bike. His legs were getting better, but he couldn't pedal as fast as usual.

I rode along, wondering if breaking into the hospital was the daftest thing I'd ever done. I might get into terrible trouble, and Mum would be furious if she found out. But anything was better than doing nothing. Wasn't it?

As we turned into Ouseley Road, the clouds parted. A pale moon broke through and we saw the hospital looming large behind the railings.

'This is it, All-Off!' I called over my shoulder and stopped at the gate. 'What do we do now?' I asked, sure he'd done this kind of thing loads of times.

He stared across at the red-brick building. 'No good trying that front door. It'll be locked at this time of night. We'll go into

149

the grounds and walk around the outside. We'll soon find a way of getting in. It's a pound to a penny we'll find a window open.'

'What then?'

'You climb in, mate. I'd do it myself but my legs ain't up to much climbing at the minute. But it should be doddle.'

'Is this where Mum is?' Rose asked in a very loud voice.

'Sssssshhhh!' I said. 'You've got to stay quiet, Rose, or someone might hear.'

We wheeled the bikes through the gate and propped them against an ivy-covered wall not far from the entrance.

We walked along the front of the hospital and round the side. 'This place is even bigger than I thought,' I said to All-Off. 'Look! There's two new blocks over there. How do we know where she is? She could be anywhere.'

All-Off stayed calm. 'Don't worry, mate. We'll try the main part first and hope we're in luck.'

The hospital had two floors with rows of tall, thin windows on each. They were all shut.

'Shame it's a cold night,' All-Off whispered. 'If it was summer they'd have left some open.'

'Well it ain't summer,' I snapped and I wondered if All-Off wasn't as clever as I thought he was. 'What are we going to do if we don't find an open window?'

'I ain't given up yet, Billy. I've got ideas, I have.'

Before I could ask him what ideas, I heard the sound of an engine. Something was heading up the drive.

I grabbed Rose's hand and pulled her over into some bushes. 'Quiet, Rose. Not a word,' I said, hugging her to me

150

as the three of us crouched among the greenery. We stayed low as an ambulance with partly covered headlights came round the corner and continued towards the back of the hospital.

'Let's follow it,' I said. 'We might find another way in.'

We stepped out of the bushes and ran across the drive, keeping low. We pressed our backs against the wall of the hospital and crept in the direction of the ambulance, which stopped some yards further on. Double doors into the building swung open and a couple of nurses hurried out.

'You stay there,' I said. 'I'm going to see what's going on.'

I dropped onto all fours and wriggled over the ground on my belly like a soldier in a battle. I watched the ambulance men lift a stretcher out of the back and carry it inside, attended by the nurses. That gave me a chance to look in through the double doors. But I soon backed off and joined All-Off and Rose.

'No good,' I said, keeping my voice low. 'Too many people coming and going. Won't be easy to get past. We'd be seen.'

We turned to go back the way we had come and kept a look-out for open windows. *Fat chance*, I said to myself as we trudged round the building. I was thinking that the whole idea was stupid and that we ought to go home when Rose tugged on my sleeve.

'Billy,' she whispered, and I bent down to hear what she had to say. 'It's open,' she said, pointing up at a small rectangular window. There were two panes. The bottom one was closed but the smaller top part was open.

I squeezed her hand. 'Well spotted, Rose,' I said and looked round at All-Off to find him grinning at me.

'Didn't I tell you we'd find one, Billy boy? Come on. I'll give you a leg up.'

He bent over underneath the window, his hands on his knees like we do when we play leap frog, and I climbed onto his back. I wobbled for a moment or two as the wind whipped round the corner, but then I managed to steady myself and pushed my head through the opening. There was a small room with a lavatory on one side and a washbasin under the window – just the thing to stand on once I'd climbed in.

'Get a move on, Billy,' called All-Off. 'My back's killing me. I can't hold you up all night.'

I gripped the window frame and began to wriggle, twisting my legs this way and that, as if I was swimming. I tried really hard but my shoulders were too wide for the opening. Though I heaved and pushed, it was no good. I was stuck.

It must have been obvious to All-Off and Rose. The next thing I felt were hands round my ankles tugging and pulling – which was very painful. But soon my shoulders snapped free and I dropped to the ground where I sat groaning and rubbing my arms.

'Are you all right, Billy?' asked Rose.

I nodded. 'Just about.' I looked up at All-Off. 'Now what?'

'I say let Rose have a go. She's small enough.'

'No!' I said. 'She's staying out here. Mum would go mad if she knew I'd let her break in. I don't want her getting into trouble.'

'I can do it!' said Rose, excited to be useful to the big boys.

All-Off looked at her and grinned. 'You ain't going to get into trouble, are yer, Rose?'

'No. Course not!' she said. I think it was just another game to her.

'We'll lift her up and help her through that small window. Then she can undo the big one and you can get in. What do you say?'

I felt that I'd already lost the argument. 'I only brought Rose cos we couldn't leave her at home by herself. I don't like it, All-Off.'

Rose tugged at my sleeve again. 'I'm nearly six and a half, Billy. I can do it.'

'See!' said All-Off. 'Don't go soft on me, mate. Let her try.'

Reluctantly, I agreed. But I still didn't like it.

All-Off lifted Rose up onto my shoulders and I gripped her sturdy legs so she wouldn't fall. I needn't have worried. She put her head through the open window and slipped through like a worm in the veg patch. One . . . two . . . and she was gone.

'Now open the big window,' I called as loud as I dared and, while Rose stood in the washbasin, she reached for the handle and turned it.

'Good girl!' I said as I watched the lower window swing slowly open.

Twenty-Six

Searching for Mum

All-Off planned to stay outside on the lookout while I went to find Mum. Rose was going to stay in the lav with the door slightly ajar keeping her eyes open for any trouble in the corridor.

'If you see anybody, Rose,' I said. 'I want you to whistle so I'll know that somebody's coming.'

Rose was a good whistler. Dad had taught both of us when we were small so I knew she could do it.

I took a deep breath, crossed my fingers and went to open the door.

'What about that black stuff on your face, Billy?' said Rose. 'Mum might be scared seeing you like that.'

I'd forgotten about the soot so I went over to the washbasin, turned on the tap and gave my face a good lathering with the piece of soap.

'That's better,' she said and handed me a towel. 'You look like you, now!'

'You'll be really quiet, won't you, Rose?' I said as I put the towel on the rail. 'And if you think you're in any danger, I want you to climb out of the window and go back to All-Off. Promise?'

She pressed her finger across her lips and nodded.

'Right,' I said and peered into the corridor, which was surprisingly empty and silent. There were notices on the wall with arrows directing visitors to Livingstone Ward, Peter Pan Ward, Emergency Ward and Nightingale Ward and I wondered which one Mum might be in.

As I hurried along the corridor I saw the name Livingstone Ward over a set of double doors and I decided to try that one. If Mum wasn't there I'd have to try another. It wasn't going to be easy, I thought. But I'd find her no matter what.

Carefully, I pushed open the doors and peered inside. The light was very dim, but I could just make out two rows of metal beds and a stove in the middle of the room. The only sounds were heavy breathing and a few snores. It would have been easy to walk straight in and look for Mum – except for one thing. Not far from the door was a desk, lit by a single lamp, with a nurse sitting writing notes.

Bad luck, Billy! I said to myself. *You can't get in without the nurse seeing you.*

I hesitated wondering what to do when somebody at the far end of the ward suddenly called out, 'Nurse!' The nurse put down her pen and hurried off to see the patient.

This was my chance. I slipped into the ward and over to the first bed to see if it was Mum. The ward was dark so I had to bend over to get a good look. The blankets were pulled up around the patient's chin so that all I could see was hair – but it was black. Definitely not Mum.

The nurse was still at the far end of the ward as I went on to the next bed. Straight away, I could see tufts of white hair poking over the blanket so I moved quickly to the third bed where the patient was snoring. It could be Mum. She snored almost as loud as Dad, I used to hear her through the bedroom wall. My heart began to beat fast as I leaned forward to get a look. I bent over until our noses were almost touching and this was when the patient's eyes suddenly shot open and stared at me. A hand clamped round my arm. I pulled back, wanting to scream out loud. But when I opened my mouth, nothing came.

'Who are you?' the patient whispered.

'I . . . I'm Billy Wilson.'

'Billy Wilson?'

Now I could see that the patient had a bushy grey beard. It definitely wasn't Mum. He released his grip on my arm and pushed himself up on his elbows.

'Fancy you being here, Billy,' he said. 'Have you still got your banjo?'

I stared at the patient through the gloom and realised it was Tommy!

'Tommy! Is it you?' I whispered. 'Are you all right?'

'It's me, Billy! And I'm all right apart from my legs. I fell down them steps in the tube. I'm lucky to be alive. But what are you doing here? You'll get into terrible trouble if they catch you.'

'I'm looking for Mum.'

'I'm sorry I didn't find her,' he said. 'It was all such a mess.'

'No one saw her come out of the tube and she wasn't at the swimming baths where they took the people who'd been killed. So I reckon she's here. But they won't tell me anything cos I'm a kid. So I climbed in through a window.'

Tommy nodded. 'They have stupid rules here, son. But you're in the wrong place. This is the men's ward.'

'Is there a ward for ladies?'

'There's one just down the corridor – Nightingale Ward – and I think there's another upstairs. A lot from tube station bombing are in there.'

'Thanks,' I whispered, 'I'll go and look.'

I was about to leave when Tommy reached out and grabbed my arm again. 'Hang on, Billy!' he said. 'The nurse is coming. You'll get caught. Hide under the bed till I tell you different.'

I flung myself onto the floor, slid under the bed and waited until I heard the nurse's shoes squeaking on the lino as she walked down the ward and back to her desk. I lay there, wondering how long it would be before Tommy told me I could get away.

The time ticked by and still Tommy gave me no signal. It seemed like for ever and I thought I might be there until morning. But then Tommy called, 'Nurse! Nurse!' which brought her hurrying over to his bed.

'What it is, Mr Bate?' she asked. 'Are you in pain?'

'No,' said Tommy, 'but the man at the end of the ward has been calling you.'

'Has he?' she said. 'I didn't hear him.'

'I didn't think you had,' he replied. 'You'd better go and see what's up.'

A moment passed as her footsteps died away down the ward. Then Tommy whispered, 'You can come out now.' I stuck my head out from under the bed. 'Off you go, son. I hope you find your mum.'

I crawled from under the bed and scurried from the room, breathing a sigh of relief that I hadn't been spotted.

Once I was in the corridor, I followed directions to Nightingale Ward, which wasn't far away. I opened the door a crack and saw that it was like the first ward with long rows of beds on either side. The nurse in charge was half way down seeing to one of the patients. If I moved fast, I might find Mum before she returned to her desk.

I hurried over to the first bed and looked at the patient. It wasn't Mum. I decided to slip under all the beds and wriggle across the floor between each one. This way no one would see me before I popped up like a worm from its hole to check each patient. I kept doing this until I reached the last bed. The nurse was so busy that night she never spotted me.

By then, I knew that Mum wasn't in that ward and I slipped out into the corridor and leaned against the wall, feeling helpless. It was a big hospital. I'd never find her.

But Tommy had said there was another ward for ladies on the first floor. Maybe she was up there. *Come on, Billy boy!* I said to myself. *Go and look! Balham boys don't give up that easy.*

So I headed for the stairs.

Twenty-Seven

Thief!

The stairs led up to a long corridor on the next floor where several more notices were fixed on the wall. General Surgical Wards 1 and 2, and Dermatology were to the right while Operating Theatres 1 and 2 and Queen Mary Ward were in the opposite direction.

I crossed my fingers and decided to try the Queen Mary Ward, following the arrows down the corridor to some double doors. When I looked in, I saw that the ward was bigger with more beds than the others and a bigger stove in the middle. There was quite a buzz about the place. A nurse was wheeling a screen to the far end and two others were attending to a patient with both legs in plaster. One lady was plastered right down to her toes and her leg was held up at an odd angle by wires and pulleys.

While the nurses were busy, I hurried over to the nearest bed, keeping low, knees bent, hoping they wouldn't spot me in the dim light. I was planning to hide under the beds like I'd done in the last ward.

The lady in the bed had a bandage covering most of her head and one eye. She was lying on her back with her mouth open and I thought she was asleep. But as I leaned over to see if it might be Mum, things changed. She suddenly sat bolt upright and started screaming. 'Nurse! Nurse! Help! Thief!'

Then chaos broke out. All the patients woke up and a nurse came hurrying up the ward to see what was wrong. Meanwhile, I managed to scuttle across to the nurse's desk and hide underneath where no one could see me. My heart was banging against my ribs as I curled up in the shadows, my eyes squeezed tight.

'What is it, Mrs Hopkins?' one nurse asked.

The lady in the first bed stopped screaming and said, 'A b-boy! H-he came in here. He came right up to my bed. I saw him.'

'Where is he? Did you see where he went?'

'No. It's too dark. Go and find him. He's dangerous. He was going to kill me!'

I heard more footsteps as another nurse arrived.

'It could be that intruder,' she said. 'The one who took the drugs from Livingstone Ward. They'll take anything they can find. It's disgraceful. I'll telephone the police right away.'

'And I'll send for the porters,' said another nurse. 'They'll sniff him out, the little wretch!'

Footsteps headed towards the door and I heard it open and close. All this time I was under the desk, shaking with fear. Things were getting desperate. I had to get out of the hospital before the police arrived.

The voices of the other nurses seemed distant now so I poked my head out from under the desk to see what was going

160

on. Although the light was very dim, I could make out two nurses standing at the bedside of the lady who screamed. Their backs were turned towards me as they talked to her. This was my one chance to get away without being seen.

I crept across the floor, pushed open the door and slipped into the corridor. No one came after me. All I had to do was to hurry back to Rose and climb out of the window.

I was almost at the stairs when I heard a noise. I stopped and listened. It was Rose's warning whistle. Somebody must be coming. Maybe the porters.

I looked around for somewhere to hide. There were several doors nearby and I opened one. A linen cupboard filled with sheets and blankets. A cupboard wouldn't do, that was the first place they'd look for me. I pushed on another door, but it was locked.

Then I saw a perfect hiding place. Right outside one of the operating theatres was a trolley with a blanket. They must have wheeled a patient on it. Underneath was a narrow shelf and if I could lie there until things had calmed down, I didn't think anyone would find me.

I had to act fast. I could hear the porters hurrying up the staircase, talking as they climbed.

'Who would have thought it, eh, Roy?' said one. 'Stealing stuff from hospitals when there's a war on.'

'I'd give him a right belting,' said another.

'It was toilet rolls he stole last week,' said a third. 'Now he's after drugs – so the nurse said.'

'We'll get him, lads. He'll wish he'd never been born.'

I was already lying on the shelf under the trolley and I'd pulled the blanket down to hide myself. The shelf was narrow and I could easily fall off if I wasn't careful, but it was too late now to find a different hiding place. I'd just have to hang on.

As I lay there, I was struck by the madness of All-Off's plan. If I was caught, I'd be taken to a police station and charged. Then what would they do with me? And what would happen to Rose?

The porters had reached the top of the stairs. 'Come with me into the ward, Stan. You two stay here. Roy, look in the cupboards. He must be hiding somewhere.'

I didn't make a sound. I hardly dared to breathe as the men walked past my hiding place in their search. At one stage, one of them sat on my trolley and lit a ciggie. He was so close I could touch him. I didn't dare move, but before long, my toes went numb and then the whole of my leg. But when the numbness turned to cramp, it hurt so bad I had to bite on my fist to stop myself crying out.

Now someone else was coming up the stairs.

'Have you found him yet?' a voice bellowed. It was the dreaded Matron.

'We've checked the other wards and the cupboards, Matron. The operating theatres are locked.'

'Very well,' she barked. 'You can come with me. And you! Move that trolley. It should never have been left in the corridor, it's blocking the way.'

There was a muttering of, 'Right, Matron,' and then I felt the trolley being pushed along and I curled my fingers round the metal legs, hanging on tight as I wondered where I was going.

I soon found out when I heard the clang of lift doors opening and the trolley was pushed inside. If I was going down to the ground floor I'd soon be back with Rose. The cramp in my leg faded as I watched the lights on the lift wall come on at G for ground floor. But the lift didn't stop. It carried on until the light came on at B for basement. Then it stopped with a jerk, the door clanged open and the trolley was pushed out onto a concrete floor.

The next part of my journey was not good. The floor was so uneven that the trolley bumped along throwing me all ways, I had to cling on for dear life or fall off and be exposed.

As the trolley was pushed through a swing door, a light came on. We stopped, then I heard the porter walk away and the light was switched off. I waited in the blackness, scared and wondering where I was. I stretched my legs to relieve the cramp but I didn't dare climb off the trolley. Not yet.

As I lay there, I soon became aware of something crawling up my legs. Over my knees. Up inside my trousers. Not one. Two, three, four! I brushed them away but more came scurrying over my skin and I couldn't stand it. I rolled off the trolley and stamped my feet on the floor to shake them off.

I couldn't see a thing. I reached out, hoping to feel my way to the door but with every step I felt a horrible crunching under my feet. I bumped into metal objects and had to change direction so many times that I didn't know whether I was going towards the door or away from it. I stood still and tried to calm myself and then I began again. Holding my arms straight out in front of me, I shuffled forward taking small steps and pushing objects out of the way until I eventually touched a wall and – Hurray! Oh boy! – I found a switch.

I pressed it. Light flickered on. Brilliant light! I was in a storeroom crammed full of trolleys and metal beds – but when I looked down, I saw that the floor was covered with a heaving mass of cockroaches, skittering out of the light and towards the skirting board. Horrified, I ran for the door and escaped into the corridor, desperately looking for a way out of the hospital.

Twenty-Eight

Help wanted!

Some way down the corridor was the lift. If I took that up to the ground floor I'd be near to Rose. But the lift would make a noise and someone would hear – nurses, porters, even the police. I didn't dare risk it.

I looked in the other direction. At the opposite end of the corridor was a door that probably led outside. I ran to it, but when I turned the handle, I found that it was locked. I needed the key. What if I couldn't open it? What would I do then?

Come on, Billy boy! I said to myself. *Stop panicking. Stay calm. You'll soon be out of here.*

I searched around and spotted a small cupboard screwed to the wall. When I opened it, there were nine hooks inside with a bunch of keys on each. This could be my chance. My hands were shaking with fear, knowing that someone might come at any minute. I took a bunch down and tried them in the lock. Some were too small. Some were too big. I tried most of the keys until, at last, I found the one that turned and the door opened.

The light from the corridor spilled outside where a metal staircase – like a fire escape – led up to ground level. Shutting the door behind me, I scrambled up the stairs into the black night. I had to wait until my eyes adjusted to the dark before I looked around, trying to decide where I was and how I would find All-Off. An ambulance came round the corner and I pressed my back against the wall until it passed. It stopped not far away by two swing doors.

Now I knew where I was – at the back of the hospital.

With my hands flat against the wall, I felt my way round to where I'd left All-Off under the window. But I couldn't see him. He definitely wasn't there.

'All-Off!' I hissed as loud as I dared.

Then came the reply from the bushes. 'Where've you been?' and All-Off emerged brushing broken twigs from his sleeves.

'Never mind,' I said. 'The police are coming. Where's Rose?'

'She's still inside.'

'Then we've got to get her out of there.'

We stood under the window. I climbed onto All-Off's back and tapped on the glass. 'Rose!' I whispered. 'Are you all right?'

Rose's face appeared on the other side of the window, grinning as she scrambled onto the washbasin. 'I'm here, Billy. Did you hear my whistle? I was waiting for you.'

'Climb out quick,' I said and she opened the bottom part of the window and slipped through. 'No time to talk. We've got to get away.'

I grabbed hold of her and lifted her down before we set off running round to the front of the hospital.

We'd left our bikes not far from the entrance and as we came near to the front door, it opened and two men came running out of the hospital. Quickly, we crouched down by the wall, afraid they might see us. They stood on the steps peering this way and that into the darkness.

'Can't see nobody out here. Can you, Roy?' said one of the men.

'Naw!' said the other. 'I reckon he's still inside. Wait till the coppers come. They'll have men swarming all over the place.'

As he spoke, a car came through the gates, screeched to a halt in front of the door and two policemen leaped out.

'Where's the rest of you?' called the man on the steps. 'I thought you'd send a dozen at least.'

'This is all we can spare,' replied the policeman. 'There's a war on, you know. Now let's go in and see if we can find this intruder of yours.'

They disappeared inside the building, slamming the door behind them. Then we quickly found our bikes and pedalled frantically out of the hospital grounds, grateful of the dark. I couldn't help thinking how near I'd come to being caught.

We were in a bit of a panic but somehow we managed to get back to Fernlea Road without any accidents and without being stopped and questioned by a warden. Sheeba gave us her usual welcome, wagging her tail and leaping up at us as we pushed our bikes down the hall. It was good to be back.

'Right,' said All-Off, sitting down in the front room. 'Now you can tell us what happened, Billy.'

'Did you talk to Mum?' asked Rose.

I shook my head. 'I got chased away. I didn't get chance to look in all the wards.' Rose's face fell and I knew how disappointed she was.

'But we'll find her soon,' I said, trying to be cheerful. 'And you were a brilliant lookout, Rose. If you hadn't whistled, I wouldn't have known those men were on the way and they'd have caught me.'

'Yes, that was good, Rose,' said All-Off. 'Billy couldn't have got away without you.'

She smiled and suddenly looked very pleased with herself. 'It's because I'm nearly seven,' she said. She must have been very tired cos, soon after, she cuddled up to Sheeba and closed her eyes.

Once she was asleep, I told All-Off what had happened: how I'd found Tommy, how I'd gone to other wards before someone saw me and I'd got away under a trolley.

'You were lucky the police didn't get you,' said All-Off.

'I know, but what was the point of it all?' I said, feeling miserable. 'I can't be certain Mum's in that hospital. She might not be. She could be anywhere. It's hopeless.'

'It ain't hopeless. That warden said she'd been taken to St James. You're not giving up, are yer?'

I shrugged my shoulders. 'I don't know. I need help, All-Off.'

'Naw! We can look after ourselves. I've been doing it for ages.'

'But what about Mum? She must be worried about us. And Dad must be wondering why he hasn't had a letter from Mum. And what if Rose's foot gets worse and she's ill?

Things can go wrong. I know somebody who died from an infected leg.'

All-Off sighed and slapped me on the back. 'You worry too much, mate.'

I shook my head. 'I'm going to talk to Gran. I know Grandad's ill, but if I tell her what's happened, she'll think of something.'

'Where does she live?'

'Up in Yorkshire. But they've got a telephone at the farm so I could ring.'

I knew it was a good idea. Gran would listen. She always said, 'If you've got any troubles you can always talk to me and your grandad.' But first I needed money for the phone. Trunk calls were expensive – two shillings and eleven pence. Where was I going to find that much?

Then I suddenly remembered.

'The biscuit tin! Mum keeps money in it. We'll go and find it in the morning, eh?'

'Sounds good,' he said. 'Now let's get some sleep.'

We slept for a couple of hours until Sheeba started whining to be let out. So the two of us got up while we left Rose to sleep on.

The kitchen was in such a terrible state, it was still a shock to see it again. Among the bricks, the broken table and the chairs was the kitchen cabinet where Mum kept the biscuit tin. It was lying on the floor, door side down, like somebody who had fallen flat on their face. We needed to turn the cabinet over. We took hold of one end each and pushed, but it took several

169

attempts before it finally flopped over with a great crashing noise and the tinkling of broken glass. Just as I expected, the glass front was smashed and everything inside it was either scattered or broken into pieces.

'Have you found the biscuit tin?' I said. 'I've only got the lid.'

When All-Off eventually discovered it under some rubble, it was battered out of shape and, worst of all, it was empty.

'Now where do I get some money?' I said.

All-Off laughed. 'We'll just look through the rubbish, Billy. The bomb won't have damaged the coins. It'll just take time to find 'em, that's all.'

He was right – it did take time. It was dirty work, sifting through broken bricks and dust and concrete. I was soon filthy and my throat was choked with dust.

I was feeling fed up. I hadn't found a single coin and I was ready to give up when All-Off shouted, 'Hey! I've got two pennies and a threepenny bit.'

This changed everything. I was back to being Billy Wilson again. Determined to find some coins for myself. I scrabbled around in a different spot, tossing stones over my shoulder, digging deeper in the debris. By the time we'd finished our search we'd found a small fortune – ten pennies, two three-penny bits, three sixpences and a shilling. We stood there on the rubble grinning at our success.

'While we're standing here,' said All-Off, 'let's look in the bottom cupboard. There might be gold dust in it!'

I laughed but it wasn't far from the truth. There were lots of tins in there – prunes, peas and evaporated milk. What a find! We were so pleased that we cheered.

All the noise had woken Rose and she came, still half asleep, and stood in the doorway. 'You look very dirty,' she said.

There was no mirror to see myself, but All-Off looked bad – so I reckoned that I must look the same. The dirt had seeped into our skin. Our clothes, which were already dirty and torn, were covered in yet another layer of dust. We looked terrible.

'We'll have a wash,' I said and we clambered over the debris to the sink and turned on the tap. The soap must have been somewhere under the rubble, so it wasn't easy to clean the dirt off. But we took it in turns to hold our heads under the running water and scrub as best we could. If that didn't do a perfect job, we rubbed off the rest of the dirt with a tablecloth we found in the sideboard.

Rose smiled. 'Now I can see your face, Billy.'

When I'd brushed some of the dust off my clothes, I was ready to go.

I turned to All-Off. 'What do you think? Am I clean enough to go to the telephone box? I don't want people thinking I'm living rough. I suppose I could go upstairs and I might find a clean shirt.'

All-Off cocked his head to one side. 'Naw! You look all right to me, Billy. You go and phone your gran while me and Rose buy a loaf of bread with some of that money. Give me five pence. That should leave you enough for the phone.'

171

'I want to go with Billy,' Rose insisted. 'I want to talk to Gran.'

We had a bit of an argument. I didn't want Rose there. I had to explain our problems to Gran and there was no time for chat. Rose had to go with All-Off. Once that was settled we put our coats on and headed for the front door.

'I suppose you know your gran's phone number, do you?' All-Off asked.

'Course I do! I've been to the phone with Mum loads of times. It's Camblesforth...' I opened my mouth to say the number but it wouldn't come. My brain had suddenly gone blank.

'Well?' said All-Off. 'Go on. What is it?'

But it was no good. I couldn't remember.

Twenty-Nine

The phone call

Sometimes my little sister can be quite helpful. That day, she really got me out of a spot of bother.

'Mum's got a book,' she said.

At first I thought she was being silly. 'What do you mean? What kind of book?'

'A little black one. She writes things in it.'

'What?'

'Addresses and phone numbers...'

Of course! 'She keeps it in the sideboard! I remember now. Thanks, Rose.'

I dashed into the front room and opened a drawer in the sideboard. There it was – small and black with the letters of the alphabet down one side. I flicked it open and found the 'W' page. Gran and Grandad's surname was Wilson like us and there, in Mum's neat writing, was their address and phone number.

'Got it!' I yelled. 'Camblesforth 49!'

We reached our coats from the hooks in the hall and set off down Fernlea Road. When we got to the end, I went one way heading for Rossiter Road while All-Off went on to the shops with Rose and Sheeba.

The telephone box was on the corner and my heart started thumping as I got near to it and I thought what I was going to say to Gran. When I stepped inside, I read the notice over the black Bakelite phone: *Please be brief . . . others may be waiting to make a call.* I looked round but there was nobody waiting.

As I took the coins out of my pocket I noticed that the black box on the wall was slightly crooked – which wasn't a good sign. I picked up the receiver and listened for the dialling tone – but there was no sound. I put the receiver down and picked it up again, hoping I'd hear it this time. Still nothing. The phone was dead.

Feeling more than a bit fed up, I pushed the door open and stepped outside. A woman carrying a shopping basket came hurrying down the street and called out, 'That phone's not working, darlin'. It's been like that for two days. I expect it's the bombing what's done it.' And she went on her way.

There was another phone box in Cavendish Road so I didn't waste any time and set off, cursing the Luftwaffe for messing up everything.

When I reached the phone box, I was relieved to see that it looked all right. No damage on the outside at least. I crossed my fingers as I stepped inside and, this time, when I lifted the receiver, I heard the dialling tone. Yes! My hands were shaking as I dialled 0 for the operator I heard her say, 'Number please?'

'Camblesforth 49.'

'Thank you, caller,' said the operator. 'Please insert two shillings and eleven pence for your three minute call.'

I pushed the right coins through the slot into the black box and, as they dropped, each one made a noise. I'd heard it before when Mum phoned. There was a different noise for each kind of coin so the operator knew if I'd paid the right amount. Clever, eh?

'Thank you, caller,' said the operator when I'd done. 'Please press button A.'

I pushed the silver button and there was the clanking of the coins as they fell into the bottom of the box. When I heard the phone ringing at the other end I nearly exploded with excitement. Any minute now I'd be talking to Gran and our troubles would be over.

It rang for some time until somebody picked up the receiver and I heard Grandad say, 'Hello?'

He must be better, I thought. *That is really good news.*

'Hello, Grandad,' I said. 'It's me, Billy. I'm really glad you're there because I wanted to tell—'

'Hello? Hello? Who is it?'

'Grandad, can you hear me? Mum's been hurt and she's in hospital but they won't let us see her.'

'Hello? You'll have to speak up. I can't hear you.'

'IT'S BILLY, GRANDAD!' I shouted down the phone so loudly that I reckoned they could hear me in the next street.

'What's that? It's a bad line,' Grandad replied.

Then I heard Gran say, 'Give me the phone, Arthur. You haven't got your hearing aid in. You shouldn't answer the

phone without your hearing aid. Now, come on, pass it over.'
There was a distant conversation between her and Grandad,
before he finally gave her the phone.

'Hello? Who is it?' asked Gran.

'Gran!' I yelled, almost as loud as before. 'It's Billy.'

'No need to shout Billy, love. Sorry your Grandad answered
the phone. He's no good without his hearing aid. But he won't
be told—'

'Gran I've got to talk to you.'

'Is something the matter, Billy?'

'Yes, Gran.'

'Is your Mum with you? Pass her the phone, love, and I'll
have a word.'

'No. Mum's in—'

This was when the pips went beep...beep...beep, telling
me that I'd used up most of the three minutes and if I wanted
to speak for longer, I'd have to put more money in the slot –
fast. I felt in my pocket and I pulled out the two coins that
were left. But they were threepenny bits. The phone wouldn't
accept them.

'What's the matter, Billy?' asked Gran. 'Is something wrong?'

'Yes, Gran. Please help us. It's Mum. She's—'

But the line suddenly went dead. I'd no money for another
call and still Gran didn't know what trouble we were in.

Thirty

Finding Feathers

When All-Off got back with Rose he poked his head into the front room where I was sitting on the settee feeling really miserable.

'It took us ages to get the bread,' he said. 'The queue was a mile long! How about you? Did you make that phone call?'

I gave him the bad news. 'Grandad answered the phone but he couldn't hear me cos he's deaf. By the time Gran came on the phone, the pips went and I'd run out of time. It was a disaster.'

All-Off raised his eyebrows in surprise. 'You mean you didn't get to talk to her?'

'Not really,' I said. 'If you've got any more money I'll try again.'

He looked at me and shook his head.

'You can always write them a letter,' he suggested.

'A letter will take days to reach them and how will we get a reply? They don't deliver post to bombed-out houses.'

There I was again, moaning and miserable. Billy Wilson thinking the worst. Feeling that everything was hopeless and that we'd never find Mum.

'But it's worth a try,' said All-Off. 'Better than doing nothin',
ain't it?'

I sort of agreed with him and so I said I'd write to Gran
later. 'Let's have something to eat first.'

Rose was out in the garden playing with Sheeba. 'Come on
in,' I called. 'All-Off's making sandwiches.'

'We queued and queued for that loaf!' she shouted from the
top end of the garden. When she came inside, she said, 'All-
Off got a tin of sardines from another shop. But I don't like
sardines.' Then she slipped her hand in mine. 'I wish we had
some eggs, Billy. I love eggs and soldiers!'

'We ain't got no chickens, Rose. No chickens, no eggs.'

'Mrs Scott's got chickens,' she said as we walked down the hall.

'But she ain't there no more.'

All-Off heard us. 'We could go and see if her chickens have
been laying,' he said.

'It don't seem right,' I said as we walked into the front room.
I didn't like the thought of stealing eggs.

All-Off turned and grinned. 'What's the harm if Mrs Scott
ain't there? I don't suppose she'd mind, would she?'

'No, I don't think she would,' I said. 'Let's go and look.' So
we clambered over the broken fence while Rose stayed behind
with Sheeba.

'Where are the chickens?' All-Off asked.

I pointed to the top of the garden. 'Mrs Scott puts 'em in the
shed every night.' But as I spoke, I noticed that the door of
the shed was open.

'Looks as if somebody's beaten us to it,' said All-Off.

There was no sign of the birds in the garden. If they were still here, I thought, they'd be pecking around looking for food.

'Somebody took 'em,' said All-Off.

I thought I knew who'd done it. 'It's probably the same kids who took our veg.'

All-Off nodded. 'Could be. I expect they were hungry and your Mrs Scott ain't here to eat the eggs, is she?'

I nodded. They were just kids living like us in bombed-out wrecks. So they stole food. And who could blame 'em?

'Come on. Let's go back inside,' I said, wanting to get away. I climbed back over the fallen fence to where Rose was waiting.

'Did you find the chickens?' she asked.

'No. They're not there.'

'But what about the eggs?'

'No eggs. Sorry, Rose. We could open that tin of prunes,' I said, trying to take her mind off the chickens. 'And you can have evaporated milk on them, if you like.'

But Rose pulled a face. 'You didn't look properly,' she said, letting go of Sheeba. 'I'll find them! I know they'll be there.' And she pushed past us and clambered into Mrs Scott's garden.

'No, Rose. They've gone!' I called as I ran after her. But she was soon at the top of the garden, and by the time I got there, she had disappeared into the shed.

'They haven't all gone, Billy,' she said, pointing to the roof where a large chicken was perched on a rafter. 'But she won't come down. I think she's frightened. Who frightened her, Billy?

179

It's not nice. Can we take her home and look after her? I'm sure Mrs Scott wouldn't mind.'

And that was how we came to have a chicken called Feathers – which was the name Rose gave her. The other four chickens had probably been stolen, but maybe this one had stayed out of reach. Clever girl!

I carried Feathers and put her in our shed. Rose followed behind clutching two eggs she had found. 'Can we cook them now, Billy?'

'We can't light a fire, Rose. Somebody might see.'

But All-Off had another idea. 'Let's use that tin bucket over there and make a fire in it. It won't make much smoke out here, I reckon. Nobody will come looking.'

It was a bit of a risk, but it was worth doing for the taste of fried eggs.

There was a sack of kindling wood and some matches in the shed. I found a frying pan in the kitchen and an old newspaper. All-Off broke some small twigs from the apple tree in Mr Wordsley's garden next door on the other side.

We crumpled the newspaper and put it in the bucket. 'That should get it going,' said All-Off, throwing in a lighted match. We put the kindling in next and then the twigs. When it was burning well, we added some bits of broken fencing and put the pan on top. Soon the eggs were sizzling and we crouched round watching them cook as our mouths watered at the thought of tasting them.

There was a chilly wind so, when the eggs were done, we carried the pan inside and dipped four slices of bread in the runny yolks. One for each of us and one for Sheeba. They were delicious and the pan was as clean as new by the time we'd finished eating. We didn't leave one bit.

Rose spent the rest of that morning in the shed feeding Feathers some chicken food she'd found in Mrs Scott's hen coop. Meanwhile All-Off and me started nailing up the fence so that Feathers would be able to peck around in our garden without anybody trying to steal her.

When we'd done, All-Off said, 'Are you going to write that letter to your Gran?'

I know I'd said I would – but I didn't think it would do any good. The post wasn't that reliable and the postman wouldn't deliver letters down our street now there was so much bomb damage. So how would I get a reply?

'Well, are you?' asked All-Off.

'Nothing to lose I suppose,' I said and I found a piece of paper and wrote down all the terrible things that had happened, ending like this:

I'm hoping you can help us, Gran. Even though Grandad's poorly. Love from Billy and Rose xxx

Then I put the letter in an envelope and copied the address from Mum's black book. Luckily, there was a stamp in the sideboard, so I stuck it on and took the letter down to the pillar box, hoping it wouldn't be long before it arrived at Gran's farmhouse.

Thirty-One

A painful landing

'People are giving me funny looks,' I told All-Off when I got back from posting the letter. 'Do you think they know I'm living rough? Maybe we need to smarten up a bit.'

All-Off looked at me, tilting his head to one side. 'You look all right to me, mate. But some people are fussy.'

'I don't want to look like I'm living on a bomb site,' I said.

All-Off shrugged. 'Well, we haven't got anything to do this afternoon. You could look around. See if you can find some clothes.'

We'd been in some filthy places. Rose didn't look good. Her skirt was torn as well as dirty – but she didn't complain. We didn't mind much what we looked like but Mum would go mad if she saw the state of us.

'All right. I'll go upstairs,' I said. 'There'll be something in the chest of drawers, I expect.'

'You'll have to watch out, Billy. The floors up there might not be safe.'

I wasn't worried. I could feel the stairs rock solid under my feet – there was no creaking or wobbling. Once I reached the top, I pushed the door open to Mum's bedroom, which was at the front of the house, over the top of the front room. So I thought that should be sound, too.

At first, when I went in and looked around, I thought that very little had changed except for a broken window and a little china dog that had fallen off the dressing table and smashed. Mum would be sad about that. Rose and me had bought it for her birthday two years ago.

Everything was covered in a thick layer of dust, of course, but dust was everywhere now. I hardly noticed it. But when I looked up at the ceiling, I was shocked. Right in the middle was a hole. Not a small hole but one that went right through the roof and open to the sky. There was more damage than I'd thought.

The large chest of drawers where Mum kept all our clothes was very old and had belonged to her mother. It had six drawers and was tall and solid and stood near the door. I opened the bottom drawer and pulled out a pair of short trousers and a shirt for me. Then I thought about All-Off. It must have been weeks since he had clean clothes. He was taller than me but maybe one of Dad's shirts would fit him. I took one from the top drawer before looking for something for Rose. When I found a grey skirt, some knickers and a pink jumper, I knew she'd be pleased.

I bundled the clothes under my arm, but before I went downstairs, I couldn't help taking a look in my bedroom. It was at the back of the house over the kitchen and this was the part with the most damage. I just needed to see if my things were still all right.

I wasn't expecting it to be perfect, but as I pushed the door open and looked inside, it was worse than I thought. Most of the back wall had gone – that was no surprise, I'd seen that from the garden. But two other walls had cracks so wide that I could push my fist into them. And there wasn't much of the ceiling left, either. Most of it was scattered across the floor.

I felt sick. This was my room! The room I had had since I was a baby. I stepped gingerly through the door and I heard the floor creak and felt it move. Nothing was safe.

In spite of the danger, there was something I needed to see. I dumped the clothes on the bed and opened the top drawer of my little bedside cabinet. There was a pile of photographs inside which were special to me. Every night I used look at them before I went to sleep. I sat on the edge of the bed and looked at them again, one by one, remembering how we'd had a picnic on Brighton beach and played on the shingle. We'd gone paddling in the sea, which was too cold for swimming, but we'd splashed about a lot and laughed a lot and had fun. I remembered it all. Then, two days later, Dad had left to join the army and nothing was much fun after that. Our family wasn't the same without him.

Clutching the snaps to my chest, I flung myself backwards on the bed and closed my eyes, feeling the springs bounce up and down and the soft mattress wrap around me. How I wished I could sleep in my own bed again instead of an air-raid shelter or a cupboard.

I was lying there, lost in my thoughts, when I heard the floor creak as if someone was walking across it. I opened my eyes and sat bolt upright. The bed and the wardrobe were juddering and the picture on the wall fell off its hook and smashed. In a panic, I tried to climb off the bed, but it was moving too much. Left to right. Up and down. Nothing in the room was still – as if the whole house was shaking.

'Help!' I yelled as the floorboards began to crack. They were no longer strong enough to support the bed and suddenly they splintered and a great hole appeared in the floor. The bed tipped towards it and I was thrown forward, still clutching the photos in my hand. Then the bed slid down into the kitchen and I fell with it. Together we crashed through the broken floorboards and into the rubble below.

It was a painful landing among the broken bricks. My legs hurt. My back. My arms. When everything stopped moving I scrambled to my feet just in time to be showered by thick dust falling from the ceiling, filling my mouth and ears. There was so much dirt that I couldn't speak. Grit scratched my eyes and made me screw them up tight. Then I heard a rumbling sound overhead. More plaster rained down and the joist, which supported the upper floor, cracked and the massive timber crashed into the kitchen, missing me by inches but trapping me against the wall.

I tried to shout to All-Off, but when I opened my mouth, I sucked in the gritty dirt and I was overcome by a coughing fit. I spat out some of the grit as my bedside cabinet fell through the hole and smashed with a deafening racket. The kitchen was a mish-mash of lumber, bricks and broken furniture. I couldn't see it, of course. I could only hear the noise and smell the dust and taste the mess of it. My eyes were squeezed shut and I couldn't move. The dust continued to fall, making me cough even more until tears rolled down my cheeks.

'All-Off,' I croaked. 'Where are you?'

'I'm here. I'll get you out, Billy,' he called. 'But don't move. You'll bring more down if you do.'

'Get me out quick!'

'I'll think of something. Don't worry, mate.'

Don't worry? It was all very well for him to say 'Don't worry'. He wasn't stuck between a bed, a beam and a wall.

'Get me out of here,' I yelled again, but there was no reply. All-Off must have gone to get help, I thought.

Once the tears had washed the grit from my eyes, I managed to open them. But I was trapped in such a small space that I couldn't move at all. I couldn't even turn my head. While I waited for All-Off, I swivelled my eyes from side to side looking at the damage as best I could. It was then that I saw something in the corner, half buried in rubble.

It was a small, unexploded bomb.

Thirty-Two

Extreme danger?

When I saw the bomb, I started to panic and I screamed as loud as I could.

'Help! Somebody come and get me! There's a bomb! Come quick before it goes off!'

I heard the crunch of All-Off's feet on the rubble.

'What happened, Billy? I was out in the shed looking for—'

'Don't waste your time!' I yelled. 'There's a bomb. If you don't get me out quick, it'll be too late.'

'A bomb. Where?'

'Over in the corner.'

I couldn't see Sheeba but I could hear her panting close by. 'Get the dog out of here or she'll set it off.'

'She's just being friendly, Billy,' I heard Rose say.

'Get away from here, Rose. That bomb could explode at any minute.'

Sweat broke out on my forehead when All-Off didn't say anything. What was he doing? I couldn't see. Was he just standing there? Why hadn't he gone for help?

I broke out into uncontrolled coughing and when I

was done, I yelled again. 'What are you doing, All-Off?...
All-Off!'

'Not much,' he said, his voice calm. 'I'm just taking a look
at it.'

I swivelled my eyes to the left and could just make out a part
of the bomb and All-Off's hand touching it!

'Are you crazy?' I screamed. 'Get away from it! Call the army.
Find somebody who knows what to do!'

All-Off didn't speak. He was brushing the debris away from
the bomb. This was madness! I expect he'd seen a film with an
unexploded bomb in it. He probably thought he knew how to
defuse one. I closed my eyes so I couldn't see anything at all.

It was the longest few minutes of my life.

Then he said, 'There!' That's all he said, 'There!' So I opened
my eyes and tried to see what he'd done. But I couldn't.

'Come and look at this, Rose,' he said. 'What do you think?'

I screamed, 'Stay where you are, Rose!' But it was too late.
I heard her scrambling over the debris.

'No, Rose,' I yelled. 'Get away! Run before it explodes!'

Then Rose began to laugh. 'Don't be silly, Billy. It's not a
bomb. It's Dad's banjo.'

I didn't believe her. 'What?' I yelled.

All-Off laughed, too. 'What you saw was a part of the banjo
sticking out of the rubbish.'

So I wasn't going to die. The relief was enormous, but I was
covered in sweat and couldn't stop shaking. Worst of all, I felt
a fool.

'Just get me out of here,' I snapped. 'I can't move an inch.'

I could tell All-Off was laughing even though he was trying to keep it quiet.

'I fetched a long ladder from the shed,' he told me.

'How's that going to help?'

'I'll prop it under that big beam to make sure it won't move. Then I'll pull you out.'

It's hard to trust somebody to get you out of a dangerous situation. But I could either let All-Off help me or I could stay trapped where I was. As I saw it, I didn't have a choice. I just crossed my fingers and hoped he could do it without bringing more of the bedroom down on my head.

Luckily Dad's wooden ladder was strong enough to stop the beam from slipping and I was soon out from under that terrible mess. I clambered over the rubble and, by some miracle, my hand was still clutching the photographs.

'Are you all right, Billy?' Rose asked. I couldn't speak. I was still learning to breathe again. 'What have you got there?' she said, pointing to the snaps.

I handed them over and she sat on a heap of bricks, smoothing the creases out of them on her knee.

'That's Dad and Mum at the seaside,' she said, staring at the first one. 'I remember that.' She looked at the others, kissing each one as she did. Then she clutched them to her chest as her eyes filled with tears. 'When do you think Dad will come home, Billy?' she asked.

'When the war's over, Rose,' I said, now I'd recovered my breath. 'We'll go to the seaside again, eh? We'll take Sheeba and we'll have a picnic. That will be good, won't it?'

She nodded and wiped her tears away with her jumper, put her arm round the dog and hugged her.

'They won't send us away, will they? I don't want to go away.'

'Neither do I,' I said. 'We won't go anywhere till Mum gets better. Then we'll all go up to Yorkshire.'

I thought about Mum a lot. But I didn't dare go back to the hospital. I wasn't even certain she was there. So how could I find her? I needed Gran and Grandad to help me, but how long would it be before they received the letter I posted that morning?

The answer was: *too long.*

Thirty-Three

A way to get money

That afternoon, we had sardines on a slice of bread for tea with some apples that were still hanging on the tree in Mr Wordsley's garden. Sheeba had found her own food that day – a rat caught in one of the traps Dad had set behind the shed. She seemed to like it cos she ate the lot.

We sat in the front room, eating our food slowly, trying to make it last. All the time, longing for some hot buttered toast, fried bacon or chips.

'Why can't we have sausage and mash?' Rose complained as she played around with the sardines.

'We couldn't cook 'em,' I explained. 'But sardines are nice, aren't they?'

She pulled a face. 'I don't like 'em,' she said, pushing the sardines away. 'I hate sardines!' Then she bent down and started tugging at her boots.

'What are you doing?'

'My foot's sore,' she said. 'I'm taking my wellies off.'

'No! Keep them on, Rose. You don't want to get dirt into that cut, do you?'

She went into a bit of a sulk and she sat there, refusing to speak. But at least she kept her wellies on.

By the time All-Off and me had finished eating, it had started to go dark. We knew it wouldn't be long before the air-raid siren started.

Rose limped outside calling, 'Come here, Feathers. It's time you were in bed.'

Feathers liked being chased around the garden, keeping clear of Rose's outstretched arms. Even Sheeba joined in the fun, racing after her and barking every now and then. But there was never any chance that she'd catch the chicken who could always flap her wings and get out of Sheeba's reach. In the end, Rose managed to scoop her up and carry her clucking and squawking into the shed.

'Don't forget to lock it,' I called. 'We don't want anyone taking her away.'

Moaning Minnie sounded early that night and we gathered our bits and pieces and called Sheeba to follow us into the cupboard under the stairs. Then we lit a small stub of candle and settled down for the night.

Rose hated to hear the German planes overhead. 'Sing, Billy,' she said. 'Play Dad's banjo.'

The banjo had somehow survived the collapse of my bedroom, only suffering some scratches and one broken string – so I could still play it, sort of.

Rose lay down, her arms around Sheeba, while I strummed on the strings and sang 'Rule Britannia' and 'Doing the Lambeth Walk'. I wasn't a brilliant singer, but All-Off joined in and it was loud enough to drown out some of the noise of war.

Once Rose had fallen asleep, we had a serious talk. The sort of stuff I didn't want my kid sister to hear.

'Do you think it's still safe in this cupboard?' I asked. 'You know...what with the bedroom floor cracking up. I was thinking the stairs might be a bit rocky after that. You don't think they'll fall down, do you?'

All-Off shook his head. 'Don't worry, Billy. I've checked round the house and the front looks solid, if you ask me. No cracks. Nothing. And the stairs are sound as a bell. They won't collapse.'

All-Off seemed confident. But was he always right? I wondered.

As if he could read my mind he said, 'If you don't feel safe here,' he said, 'we could go and look for another place tomorrow. We might find a house with a nice cellar and loads of food. That would be brilliant.'

'No, it wouldn't!' I snapped. 'Me and Rose are staying here till Mum gets back. You go if you want, but we're staying.'

All-Off seemed upset. 'I ain't going nowhere without you, Billy. I just thought you might like a change. This place ain't up to much, is it?'

Now it was my turn to feel offended. 'You might think it's just a load of rubble, but this is our home and we ain't leaving it. Not without Mum anyway.'

I sat there, my head in my hands, feeling bad. Nothing was going right. Dad was away fighting the Nazis, Mum was goodness-knows-where and everybody wanted to send us away. Nobody ever asked me what I wanted. If they did I'd tell 'em that I wanted my family back again. Mum, Dad, Rose and me. Back to normal.

'Why don't you phone your gran again tomorrow if it'll make you feel better.'

I felt like hitting him. 'Are you stupid, or what? Where am I going to find the money? I haven't got any.' I turned away, shaking with anger.

All-Off tapped my arm. 'I can get money.'

I glared at him. 'Oh yeah? How? Do you go thieving or something?'

He laughed. 'Naw! Not me, mate.'

'Then how?'

'I can sell things.'

'Like what?'

'I reckon I could sell your banjo. I know a chap who'll buy it.'

'No! That banjo was Dad's. He gave it to me. I'm learning to play a tune for him when he comes home. I promised.'

All-Off thought for a minute. 'Well the only other thing is your bike. You'd get a good price for that and we could buy some food.'

'I can't. Dad bought that bike from Mrs Chitterlow. It was my birthday present.'

All-Off nodded. 'I suppose selling the bike ain't a good idea. A bike's too useful. But I bet your Mum's got some clothes we could get good money for?'

194

'No! Mum'll need them when she comes home.'

I thought for a minute. 'What about selling a garden fork or a spade?' I suggested.

'Don't think we'd get much for 'em. Just a few pennies.'

In the end, I couldn't think what else to do so I agreed to sell Dad's banjo. I felt bad, as though I was letting him down – even though I knew he'd understand that I was desperate for money.

That night, we listened as wave after wave of German planes flew overhead. I was kept awake by the noise and the terrible fear that at any minute a bomb might drop on us. But no bombs fell on Balham and, once the All Clear had sounded, my eyelids grew heavy and I fell asleep, knowing that we were safe for another day.

Thirty-Four

Meeting Mrs Chitterlow

'Right,' said All-Off the next morning. 'Let's go to the music shop at the top of Cavendish Road. I know Mr MacKeith. He's a good old chap. He collects musical instruments, see. He'll buy it for a fair price, I know he will.'

With a heavy heart, I took the banjo out of the cupboard under the stairs. It felt like parting with a little bit of Dad. I tucked it under my coat as we set off. It was raining and I didn't want it to get wet.

As we walked down Fernlea Road, we passed the houses I'd known since I was small. They belonged to people I'd known. Boys I'd played football with. Now, after the bombing, they were wrecked and I tried to turn my head away – but it was no use. It was the same wherever I looked.

'Why are we taking the banjo, Billy?' Rose asked as she walked beside us with Sheeba on the lead. And when I explained, she stood stock-still and glared at me.

'No, Billy! You can't sell it! That's Dad's banjo. He said you had to look after it!' And she folded her arms across her chest, clamped her lips tight together, and refused to move. It was some time before we persuaded her to get going. Even then she walked several paces behind saying that she didn't want to come cos her foot hurt. At least that was her excuse.

We had just turned into Cavendish Road when I saw Mrs Chitterlow heading towards us, carrying her shopping basket. She was married to a friend of Dad's called Herbert and they'd joined the army together.

'Hello!' she said as she came nearer. 'It's Billy, isn't it?'

I nodded.

'How do you like your bike, dearie?'

'It's smashing, thanks, Mrs Chitterlow. It was a great birthday present.'

'My Herbert would be ever so pleased to know that you've got it,' she said.

I thought she looked a bit sad when she said that and I wondered where Mr Chitterlow was now – but I didn't like to ask.

'How's your mother managing with your dad away?' she said.

Now this was a problem. I couldn't tell the truth so I said, 'She's fine thanks. She's working at Mr Lodey's garage.'

Luckily Rose was some way off, still sulking.

'Well,' said Mrs Chitterlow, 'I must say I'm surprised you children are still in Balham. My kids were evacuated months ago.' Then she sighed. 'I miss them something shocking. I can't wait to have them back.'

Rose came and stood next to me and looked up at her.

'I'm guessing you're Billy's sister?'

Rose smiled and nodded. 'I'm Rose,' she said. 'And I'm nearly seven.'

'And where are you going this morning?'

Rose couldn't wait to tell her. 'We're going to sell Dad's banjo so we can buy some food. But I don't think we should. Billy's got it under his coat. Look.' And she tugged my coat open.

Mrs Chitterlow's eyes flashed wide in surprise. 'You're going to *sell* it?' she said. 'Are you sure your dad would want you to, Billy? He loved playing his banjo. My Herbert always said how good he was.'

I couldn't stop Rose.

'We haven't got any money for sausages if we don't sell it,' she said. 'And I'm really hungry and—'

All-Off suddenly butted in. 'Billy lost the money his mum gave him before she went to work. It was three shillings to do some shopping.'

Mrs Chitterlow's mouth fell open as he told her this fanciful story. I grabbed hold of Rose and held her tight in case she said it was all a lie.

'I must have dropped it somewhere,' I added. 'We looked but we couldn't find it and we didn't know what else to do. Mum's going to be really angry when she finds out. That's why we're going to Mr MacKeith's music shop.'

'But you can't, dearie,' said Mrs Chitterlow. 'It was bombed two nights ago.'

Our faces must have shown how shocked we were.

But a smile soon spread across Mrs Chitterlow's face. 'Bless you! You are in a pickle, aren't you?' Then she took her purse out of her basket. 'My children are a long way from home and if they were in trouble, I hope somebody would help them. So I'm going to give you some money.' She opened her purse and counted out four sixpences and twelve pennies into my hand. 'Three shillings exactly,' she said. 'There! Now you won't need to sell your dad's banjo and you can do that shopping.' She winked at us. 'And I won't say a word to your mother.'

'Thanks, Mrs Chitterlow,' I said, amazed at this piece of luck. 'Thanks very much. I'll pay you back as soon as I can.'

Only Rose stood there looking puzzled not quite sure what was going on. I didn't feel good about telling lies, but if it meant I could make that phone call, maybe it wasn't such a bad thing.

Once Mrs Chitterlow had gone off to do her shopping, I said. 'Let's go to the phone box now. It's not far up the road.'

When we reached it, Rose begged me to let her speak to Gran. 'Not this time, Rose,' I said. 'But I expect we'll be seeing them soon. You'd like that, wouldn't you?'

She was near to tears but All-Off got her to play hopscotch on the pavement. Good old All-Off.

I stepped inside the phone box, picked up the receiver and dialled 0 for the operator.

'Number please,' she said.

'Camblesforth 49,' I said.

'Insert two shillings and eleven pence, caller.'

Just as before I put the coins into the slot and pressed button A.

The phone rang at the other end and I waited for someone to pick up the receiver. I waited and waited, listening to that ringing tone, but nobody answered.

The operator came onto the line. 'I'm sorry, caller,' she said. 'There's no reply. Please press button B to get your money back.'

Thirty-Five

A knock on the door

When I told All-Off that nobody had answered the phone, he said, 'Look on the bright side! We've got three shillings. We could go and buy some food and we'd still have some left for the rest of the week.'

'No!' I yelled. 'We're not spending it. I need—'

But Rose was hungry. 'You promised,' she interrupted. 'You said we could buy something nice to eat.'

'No, Rose. I need that money to phone Gran later. I expect she was out shopping.'

But if she was shopping, I thought, why hadn't Grandad answered the phone? Maybe he was asleep. Maybe he just hadn't heard it ringing.

When we got back home, we were surprised to find Feathers in the kitchen. Instead of pecking around in the garden, she was perched on top of the broken cabinet in the rubble and debris. She'd settled herself down there and looked very content.

'I think she's laying an egg,' said Rose, reaching over the broken bricks to stroke her. 'That's good. We can have it for tea.'

Rose stayed with Feathers while All-Off and me went into the front room. He put what was left of the loaf on top of the sideboard and began to slice it. I was opening the last tin of Spam when there was a loud knocking on the front door. It was the sort of knocking that tells you something bad is going to happen. I just knew it.

I raised my finger and Sheeba sat silently, her eyes fixed on me. I stared at All-Off. Neither of us spoke, but I guess we were both thinking the same thing. Then Rose came into the front room clutching Feathers to her chest.

'Shhh!' I hissed before she could speak, and she stood still.

I crossed over to the window, knees bent, keeping low. I raised my head a few inches over the sill and looked out. Two people were standing by the front door. One was a tall lady in a green uniform who I recognised at once. It was Mrs Bartley who had taken us to the shelter in the school. The other was a policeman. Bad news!

I turned back to All-Off and Rose. 'Go under the stairs,' I whispered. 'They've come to get us.'

There was more knocking and the man shouted, 'Police! Anybody home?'

Rose was already in the cupboard and All-Off took Sheeba inside while I quickly pushed the bread and Spam into a drawer. If I'd left them, they'd be a dead give-away that we were living here.

The policeman rattled the doorknob and the front door swung open. But by the time he'd stepped into the hall, I was hidden with the others.

We sat there clinging together as footsteps sounded in the hall and came nearer. Then I heard them pass the cupboard heading for the kitchen. They walked around the ground floor, with Mrs Bartley calling, 'Hello! Is anybody there?'

'As you can see, ma'am,' the policeman said at last. 'There's nobody here.'

'I suppose you're right, officer. This house is a complete wreck. They couldn't be living here, could they?'

'You'd be surprised how kids manage when they need to,' the policeman replied. 'I've seen 'em in bomb sites and down in cellars. They find food wherever they can.'

Mrs Bartley sighed. 'This is terrible. Surely Billy and his sister couldn't be living among this rubble? It's too awful to think about.'

'Well,' said the policeman, 'if they *have* been living here, they've gone now. There's no sign of 'em.'

'Then where are they?' asked Mrs Bartley. 'After they'd jumped off the lorry I thought they'd come back here. I'm desperate to get them to somewhere safe.'

'You said somebody spotted them yesterday?'

'Yes. She said they looked very dirty and there was a boy with a shaved head with them.'

The policeman grunted. 'I've seen him around. He's a tough one, he is.'

'That's All-Off, as he calls himself,' Mrs Bartley replied. 'He's a clever boy. He's been living rough for some weeks and he really needs help. But he always slips out of our grasp.'

'Scoundrel, if you ask me, ma'am. But he's not here, is he? So we'd best be off. I've got things to do and I expect you have, too.'

We heard their footsteps heading down the hall. Then the front door slammed shut and we all breathed a sigh of relief.

'They've gone,' I said. 'We can get out now.'

I was surprised when Rose let out an ear-splitting howl.

'What's the matter?'

Her mouth was contorted into a horrible shape and she began to sob. 'F-F-Feathers,' she said, putting the bird on the floor. Then she opened her hand flat and revealed a broken egg, the yellow yolk dripping through her fingers. 'I broke her egg. I was saving it and I broke it.'

'Well, that's a good thing for Sheeba,' I said. 'Look! She's licking it up!' Sheeba ate the lot, eggshell and all.

I took Rose into the kitchen and washed her hand under the tap.

'Have those people gone, Billy?' she asked, still sobbing.

I nodded. 'Yeah. Course they have. There's nobody here.'

But she kept on crying.

'What's wrong?' I asked. 'You're not worried about that policeman, are you?'

'No,' she croaked. 'It's my foot.'

'Does it hurt?' I asked and she nodded. 'You're not just pretending?'

She shook her head and I bent down, pulled off her wellie then carefully unwrapped the towelling I'd put over it.

'Let's get her onto the draining board,' said All-Off and we lifted her up so that I could hold her foot under the running tap.

'Owwwwwww!' she yelled. 'Stop it, Billy!'

When I looked at the cut, I soon saw why she was shouting. The area round it was swollen and red and in the middle was a patch of runny, yellow puss. Instead of healing, the cut was infected and getting worse. She needed to see a doctor. All I could do was clean it again.

'Mum's got some serviettes in the front room,' I told her. 'We can use one as a bandage.'

All-Off stayed in the kitchen with her while I went and fetched two serviettes out of the sideboard drawer. They should have been white but they were covered in a layer of grey dust. Keeping things clean among all the bomb damage was almost impossible.

When I returned to the kitchen, All-Off said, 'I'll go and finish the sandwiches while you see to that cut.'

I dried Rose's foot as carefully as I could while she squealed and groaned. Then I wrapped one of the serviettes round it.

'How's that?' I asked as I lifted her down off the draining board, but she screwed up her face in pain when she tried to put her foot on the floor.

'It's still sore, Billy. It hurts.'

I carried her into the front room and sat her on the settee.

'All-Off's making some sandwiches,' I said. 'Do you want one?'

She shook her head. 'I'm not hungry.'

Even so, All-Off made three Spam sandwiches and we left Rose's on the sideboard in case she wanted it later.

Sheeba came and sat near her, licking her hand gently. Although the front room wasn't at all warm, I noticed that Rose's cheeks were flushed pink. When I put my hand on her forehead and it felt hot and damp with sweat.

'Lie down, Rose,' I said. 'You have a nice sleep and you'll soon feel better.'

She didn't argue. She just closed her eyes while I covered her with a blanket. Sheeba rested her chin on the edge of the seat and watched over Rose as if she knew she wasn't well.

'I'm worried,' I said to All-Off. 'That cut's much worse. She needs proper treatment.'

'Maybe,' said All-Off. 'But let's wait till she wakes up. My mum always said that sleep can work wonders.'

'And what if it doesn't? What if she gets worse? My Dad's brother died from a cut that got infected.'

All-Off rubbed his forehead. 'If she gets worse, we'll have to take her to the hospital,' he said. 'It's the only thing to do.' Then he paused for a second. 'But I'm warning you – they'll soon find out you're on your own, Billy. They'll know there ain't no grandad looking after the two of you. As sure as eggs is eggs, some official will send you off to somewhere miles away.'

I hung my head in defeat. 'I know. But I can't do anything else, can I?'

All-Off put his hand on my shoulder. 'You're my mate, Billy, and I'll help you get Rose to the hospital. But you know I can't go in. If they find out I'm on my own, they'll send me away. I'm staying in Balham till the war's over in case Dad comes back. Sorry, pal. I'll have to leave you.'

Feeling more miserable than ever, I sat and watched over Rose while she slept. For over an hour I watched, hoping that when she woke, she would be better, but deep down knowing that she would not be.

Thirty-Six

Back to the hospital

Rose was still sleeping when something else happened. There was another knocking on the front door. *Rat-a-tat*. A lead weight landed in my stomach. The police were back.

I held up my finger to Sheeba then I looked across at All-Off. He nodded towards the cupboard under the stairs.

'I'll carry Rose,' he whispered and he went to pick her up off the settee. But Rose let out a pitiful cry as if she was in real pain.

I put my hand on his arm. 'No!' I said. 'Leave her. There's no point in hiding any more.'

He raised his eyebrows as if he couldn't believe what I'd said.

'You go if you want to, All-Off. Run away if you don't want to be found. But I've had enough. Rose is ill and I've got to get her to hospital.'

After all our efforts to stay in Balham, they'd finally got us. We'd escaped from a lorry, walked across London and lived among bomb damage. All for nothing. Now the only thing that mattered to me was making Rose well again.

Rat-a-tat. Rat-a-tat. Someone hammered at the door again and a man shouted, 'Anybody home?'

Reluctantly, I walked out of the front room and down the hall. I was shaking, knowing this was the end for me and I'd be sent away.

As I opened the door, I lowered my eyes, not wanting to face the police. Then someone said, 'Well, that's a fine sight and no mistake. But you could do with a good wash, Billy!'

I looked up. It wasn't a policeman at all. It was Gran standing there in her best coat and hat with a blue scarf tied round her neck. She flung her arms wide and hugged me until I could hardly breathe, but I was suddenly filled with happiness.

Gran wasn't alone. Standing behind her was a man in a tin helmet wearing an armband with the letters ARP on it.

'This is Mr Tooley,' she explained. 'He helped me when I arrived in Balham. I wasn't sure where to go. Everything looks very different with all the bombing.' She sighed. 'I was shocked, I must say. But he very kindly showed me how to get here.'

The ARP man smiled and nodded. 'I'm glad it's worked out well for you, missus. You've found your grandson after all.'

'Thank you for your help, Mr Tooley,' said Gran. 'We'll be all right now. I expect I'll be taking them all back to Yorkshire.'

'Then if you don't mind, missus, I'll be on my way.'

Gran shook his hand and thanked him again.

'If you need any more help,' he said, 'just come to the ARP depot and we'll see what we can do.'

Mr Tooley walked away down the road and Gran stepped inside.

'I'm dying for a cuppa, Billy,' she said.

'Sorry, Gran. I can't make one,' I said.

Gran laughed. 'Then I'll just have to make my own, won't I?' She marched down the hall and pushed open the door into the kitchen.

'Oh, goodness gracious!' she cried and clapped her hands to her cheeks. 'What a mess! Dear me! There's nothing left of your kitchen, Billy.' She turned to look at me, her eyes wide. 'The house didn't look bad from the front. This is terrible. But where's your mum and Rose?'

'I think Mum's in hospital and Rose is poorly in the front room.'

'Poorly?' Gran asked. 'How poorly?'

When we went into the front room, Gran leaned over Rose and laid her hand to her forehead. 'The poor mite's burning up,' she said, shaking her head. 'She's got a terrible temperature.'

'She cut her foot on some shrapnel,' I said. 'It's infected.'

She carefully unwrapped the serviette and looked at the cut. Rose didn't wake up.

'This is really bad, Billy. We need to get her to hospital, sharpish.'

'That's what we thought, missus,' said All-Off, following us into the front room. 'We was waiting till she woke up, see.'

I was astonished to see him. I thought he'd wanted to get away, but he'd probably changed his mind when he heard it was Gran and not the police.

'Oh, good heavens!' asked Gran, surprised to see an extra boy. 'Who's this?'

'This is All-Off,' I said. 'He's a friend and he's been helping us.'

'All-Off! That's an unusual name!' said Gran. 'And it's not often I meet somebody with less hair than my husband.' All-Off grinned. 'Now, how about helping us to get this child to hospital? She can't walk, can she? So how can we get her there?'

'I know!' I said. 'Mrs Scott next door has a pram for the twins. It'll be big enough for Rose and we can push it up to the hospital.'

'Good lad,' said Gran. 'Then you two had best go and ask Mrs Scott if you can borrow it.'

I explained that Mrs Scott's house had been bombed like ours but I didn't think she'd mind at all if we used the pram in an emergency. I knew she kept it in the hall and when All-Off and me went round we found that the door was so badly damaged we could push it open and walk in.

'That's just the job!' said Gran when we took it round to our front door. 'I'll lift Rose into it and we'll be off. I expect you know the way to the hospital.'

She went back into the front room and picked up Rose off the settee. For a second, she opened her eyes and when Gran gave her a kiss on her cheek, she smiled then fell back into a deep sleep.

Rose was a bit too big for the pram, so her feet dangled over the edge. But Gran said, 'Never mind. We'll put a blanket over her and she'll be right as rain.'

We shut Sheeba in the front room and then we set off. All-Off said he'd push the pram for a bit while Gran and me

211

walked behind and had a good chat. We couldn't walk fast as Gran suffered from rheumatism in her legs and she had to go slowly.

'You'd better tell me what's been happening, Billy,' she said and I explained how we'd lost Mum when the bomb fell on the underground and how we'd been living on our own ever since. Gran listened without saying much, but I could tell she was shocked.

'I think Mum was taken to the hospital – St James – the one we're going to now,' I said. 'I went there two days ago, but they wouldn't even tell me if she was there for certain. And they wouldn't have let me see her if she was. They don't let kids into the hospital. It's the rules, they said.'

'It's shameful, Billy, being treated like that. It was only natural you wanted to see your mum. I'll have something to say about that. Mark my words!'

I didn't mention that I'd climbed in through a window after dark. I thought Gran had had enough surprises for one day.

'So your poor mother's missing and you children are all by yourselves,' she said. 'I'm ashamed to say I didn't realise how bad things were down here. I was spending all my time rushing to the hospital – I was that worried about your grandad after his heart attack. And then there was the farm to look after. I didn't have a minute to think about anything else. I'm so sorry.' She pulled out a hankie and wiped away a tear.

'Don't be upset, Gran,' I said. 'We managed all right.'

'I just wish I'd known how hard things were for you,' she said, shaking her head. 'Thank goodness you rang, Billy.'

All-Off looked over his shoulder. 'I don't get it. I didn't think you spoke to your gran, Billy?'

'Well, he didn't have time to say much before the pips went,' Gran told him. 'But I heard him say, "Please help us, Gran" before we were cut off – and I know my grandson wouldn't ask for help unless it was something serious.' She turned to me and smiled. 'Your grandad said I should come down and see what's up – so I packed a bag and left as soon as I could.'

'Is Grandad all right, Gran?' I asked. 'Is he better now?'

'He's better than he was, love. He's staying with his friend, Frank, till I get back.'

So that explained why no one answered when I'd phoned that morning.

As we walked behind All-Off, I was hoping we'd see Mum at the hospital – once we'd found a doctor for Rose, of course. Mum had to be there, didn't she? The warden at the swimming baths said injured people had gone to St James. He had to be right. But just in case, I crossed my fingers for luck.

When we arrived at the hospital, Gran went ahead of us up the steps.

'Are you going now, All-Off?' I asked, knowing he was nervous of getting caught by some official or other.

But he just shrugged. 'I'll help you with the pram. You'll never manage it by yourself.' So All-Off and me struggled to pull the pram up the steps and in through the main door.

Gran was already at the reception desk. 'My name's Mrs Emma Wilson,' I heard her say. 'My granddaughter has shrapnel wound in her foot and it's infected. She's very poorly and needs to see a doctor right away.'

As we pushed the pram over to the desk, the receptionist raised her eyebrows and held up her finger. 'Wait there,' she said. 'I'm phoning for assistance.'

Before long a white-coated doctor came hurrying down the corridor with a nurse by his side. They went straight over to the pram. 'Poor child,' the doctor said, pressing his stethoscope to Rose's chest. 'You did right to bring her. I'll take her down to the children's ward at once. Don't worry. She'll be well taken care of.'

As they disappeared with the pram, the receptionist filled in a form while Gran gave her Rose's name, address and date of birth.

When she'd finished, Gran said, 'I believe my daughter-in-law, Mrs Ruby Wilson, is in your hospital. We should like to see her, if you please.'

The receptionist frowned, her mouth twisted as if she'd sucked on a lemon. 'I'm afraid that won't be possible,' she said. 'It's not visiting time and, anyway, we don't allow children in the hospital.'

Gran straightened her back and pulled herself up to her full height (which wasn't much!). 'Mrs Wilson is their mother,' she said. 'They ought to be able to see their own mother, surely?'

The lady behind the desk sniffed and closed her eyes for a second. 'It's the rules. Hospital rules. Children have to wait outside.' And she flapped her hand in the direction of the door.

'Then your rules don't make sense,' said Gran, gritting her teeth and thumping her fist on the desk. 'What rule says that you can treat children cruelly by keeping them away from their mother? Can you tell me what rule that is?'

The receptionist inhaled sharply and blushed. Although she tried to speak, she was so nervous of Gran she could only stutter. 'I-I'll have to g-go and find somebody,' she said and hurried away.

I tugged Gran's hand. 'One of the wards for ladies is upstairs, Gran. I think that's where Mum might be. Come on, I'll show you.'

Without waiting for the receptionist to return, we all set off down the corridor, past the door of the toilet where we'd hidden and on up the staircase, ignoring the puzzled stares of nurses and doctors. All-Off was still with us and I was glad.

'Mum might be in there,' I said, pointing to the Queen Mary Ward. I hadn't had time to go in that ward but I hoped that's where we'd find her.

Gran marched down the corridor and pushed open the double doors. It was around two o'clock by then and the ward was busy. The nurses were checking temperatures, changing dressings and giving out medicine.

As I glanced around the room, my eyes were drawn to the far end, beyond the nurses and the other patients. There was no mistaking what I saw. A patient was sitting up in bed. Her head was bandaged and she had one leg in plaster. But there was no doubt about it. It was Mum and I thought my heart would burst.

I went crazy, racing down the ward, pushing past nurses and trolleys, shouting, 'Mum!' at the top of my voice before flinging myself onto her bed.

'Billy!' she cried, holding out her arms to hug me. 'Where have you been? I've been out of my mind with worry. They said they'd tried to evacuate you but you'd run away. Is that right?'

I nodded, but I didn't want to say more. Not yet. I was too happy that I'd found her.

'A WVS lady came to see me this morning, Billy. She'd been to our house looking for you, but you weren't there. I've been frantic not knowing where you were.'

By then Gran had arrived at her bedside with All-Off tagging along behind.

'It's good to see you, Ruby,' Gran said as she bent over to kiss Mum's cheek. 'Your kids have been worried to death about you. They didn't know where you were. But when you hear how they managed by themselves, you'll be proud of them.'

Mum looked beyond Gran and saw All-Off. 'Who's this?' she asked. 'And where's Rose?'

Before I could answer, we were surrounded by nurses. They made a real fuss and tried to shoo us away. I don't suppose they wanted kids like us dirtying their wards. But it had taken me a long time to find Mum and I refused to move. Then that awful matron burst through the door and came marching towards us looking as fierce as Adolf Hitler himself.

'What's going on here?' she bellowed in that terrifying voice of hers. Everybody – patients and nurses as well as us – spun round to face her with looks of horror on their faces. 'Children are not allowed in my wards. We have rules!' She looked directly at Gran, 'And you should have waited until visiting time. Now please leave at once.'

I didn't think Gran would put up with that.

'There's no need to be rude,' she said, and the dragon looked surprised that an old lady, who was only five feet tall, would answer back. 'There's a war on, you know,' Gran continued, 'and we all have to help each other. We're here to help these children's mother and we are not leaving.'

Matron's cheeks flushed pink and it looked as though there might be a bit of an argument, except that a man in a white jacket walked into the ward with none other than Mrs Bartley.

'Good afternoon, Matron,' he said, walking over to Mum's bed. 'Is something the matter?'

'Indeed, Dr Frank,' Matron said, puffing out her chest. 'I have asked these people to leave the ward. It's against regulations. It's not right to have children in here, as you know.'

Dr Frank smiled. 'Well, this looks like a special circumstance to me, Matron. My patient has been worrying about her children. She didn't know where they were.'

'That is no concern of mine,' snapped Matron.

'Mrs Bartley here has been looking for them,' the doctor continued, 'and I'm delighted to see that the children are here and in fine health. Splendid! Splendid!'

'Dr Frank—' Matron attempted to interrupt, but the doctor held up his hand.

'I think they should be allowed to stay for a little while. I'm sure it will do the patient a power of good.' He put his hand on Matron's shoulder. 'What do you say, Matron? Half an hour with her family will be better than any medicine, don't you think?'

Dr Frank's charm seemed to work and Matron finally agreed. 'Half an hour,' she said, 'and no more.'

That was how I got to spend time with Mum. She asked about Rose and we told her what had happened. A kind nurse went down to the children's ward and came back with good news. 'Rose is awake and the doctor says she'll be much better in a couple of days.'

'Can I see her?' Mum asked.

'Yes, but leave it until later. She needs to rest now.'

Mum felt better for knowing Rose was going to be all right. After that, we talked twenty to the dozen, laughing and telling silly jokes. Gran said how sorry she was she hadn't come sooner and how well Mum had managed in the bombing.

'You're a wonderful mother, Ruby,' she said. 'Nobody could have done more for these children.'

'She's very brave, too,' said a nurse, plumping up her pillows. 'Did you know she saved a lady and her two babies down in that underground station?'

'Mrs Scott!' I said. 'Is she all right? And the twins?'

'I believe they are getting stronger every day,' she said.

I felt really proud of Mum helping somebody else to get to safety. She deserved a medal!

When the half hour was up, I gave Mum the photographs out of my coat pocket and she seemed really pleased to have them.

'Oh, that's lovely,' she said. 'It'll be the next best thing to having you with me.' As she gave me a hug she whispered in my ear, 'I'm proud of you, Billy. You took good care of Rose just like you promised Dad. But now you must promise me that when Rose is better, you'll go to Yorkshire with Gran.'

I pulled away. 'But, Mum, I don't want to go without you.'

She gripped my arms. 'Promise me, Billy. I want to know that you're safe.'

Thirty-Seven

Leaving

I was sad to leave Mum but I tried to cheer myself up by thinking that it wouldn't be long before we were all together again.

As we walked along the corridor and down the stairs, Gran chatted to Mrs Bartley.

'I don't know where we're going to sleep tonight, I'm sure,' she said. 'I arrived from Yorkshire this morning and found my grandchildren living in a bombed-out house. You've never seen such a place.'

'It's not that bad, Gran,' I said. 'We made it quite cosy. And All-Off helped us.'

All-Off looked at me and grinned. I expect he was glad I'd said that.

'Cosy or not,' Gran replied, 'we can't stay there tonight, love. Not with all them bombs dropping. We need somewhere safe.'

Mrs Bartley agreed. 'I know a safe place,' she said. 'It's not far from here. I'll take you there and you can go back to the hospital tomorrow and see how Rose and your daughter-in-law are doing.'

Gran looked very pleased. 'It will be grand to lie down and sleep properly,' she said. 'I spent all last night on the train.'

Mrs Bartley took us to a special shelter for people whose houses had been bombed. It was in a church hall and there was a great smell of food, which made me realise how hungry I was.

There were ladies in green uniforms, like Mrs Bartley, and they'd cooked up a brilliant meal of vegetable stew and dumplings with bread pudding and custard to follow.

Mrs Bartley sat with us while we ate and we talked a lot.

'That was fantastic,' I said as I spooned the last bit of custard off my plate. 'I'm full to bursting!'

'Yeah,' said All-Off who was sitting at the far end of the table. 'Great stew. Great pudding. Thanks.'

Mrs Bartley stared at All-Off. 'We've met before, haven't we?'

'Well, I've been here once or twice,' he said, looking kind of sheepish.

She smiled. 'I thought I'd seen you. Will you be going up to Yorkshire with Billy and Rose?'

All-Off shook his head. 'Them country places don't suit me. I'd rather stay here.'

Mrs Bartley frowned. 'That's not a good idea. We'll have to see about that.' Then she stood up. 'I have to go now, but the ladies will show you where to sleep,' she said. 'I'll be back at nine o'clock tomorrow and we'll see if Rose is well enough to travel. Then I'll organise some transport to take you to Kings Cross to catch your train.'

Once Mrs Bartley had gone, All-Off persuaded the ladies to give him another helping of stew.

'I'm a growing lad!' he joked and they filled his plate again. All-Off was like that! He could persuade people to do anything for him.

'You still hungry then?' I asked.

'Naw!' he said, giving me a wink. 'It's for Sheeba. I bet she's ready for something to eat. We can get to Fernlea Road before it goes dark.'

Gran didn't like the idea at first.

'If you won't let us spend the night in our house, Gran,' I said, 'we've got to go and feed Sheeba, haven't we?'

In the end, she let us go. 'But there's to be no messing about,' she said. 'Go straight home. Feed the dog. And then come back. Promise?'

'I promise.'

When we got there, Sheeba was really pleased to see us. She'd made a comfy bed for herself on the settee and Feathers was perched on a pile of rubble in the kitchen.

'We'll all be going to Yorkshire soon,' I told Sheeba and she wagged her tail as if she understood what I was saying.

Once we'd fed the dog and the chicken, we went back to the church hall where the WVS ladies were waiting for us. 'Please come and collect your blankets, boys. We'll take you and your grandma over to the shelter. The siren will be going off before long.'

Everything was well organised. Blankets were piled up on a table and we took one each and followed a WVS lady out of the hall towards the shelter in the old church. The light had already faded and she switched on her torch as we followed her through the churchyard, past the gravestones. I couldn't help remembering all those people at the swimming pool. The ones who'd died in the bombing. They were someone's mum, someone's dad. A brother or a sister. And I thought that they'd soon be buried beneath the ground. Maybe in a graveyard like this one.

'There's a crypt under the church that makes an excellent shelter,' the lady told us. 'It's not big, but there are lamps down there and some mattresses. I think you'll be comfortable.'

She led us to a door on the side of the church and opened it. 'Mind how you go,' she called over her shoulder as we followed her. 'These steps are very steep.'

Stone steps led down to a kind of cellar where another family was already settling down for the night – a mum, three small children and a baby. She was telling the older ones a story while she rocked the baby to sleep.

After the WVS lady left, we spread our blankets on the mattresses and sat on them. We hadn't been down there long before Moaning Minnie set off whining and German planes came roaring overhead as they did most nights. The baby didn't like it at all and started crying. Then the other kids joined in, and there was a right racket as the noise echoed off the stone walls.

'I'm not surprised they're scared,' said Gran. 'I don't feel so good myself.'

The mum with the baby looked across at Gran. 'It ain't very

nice down here. My kids don't like it. They think there's ghosts, see.'

'That's all just silly nonsense,' said Gran. 'There's no such thing as ghosts. You tell 'em.'

We decided that Gran should have one mattress and All-Off and me would share another, but it was a long time before those kids quietened down so we could sleep.

'I wish Sheeba was here,' I said, looking at Gran. 'She'll be going with us to the farm, won't she?'

'Well . . .' said Gran.

'And what about Feathers?' asked All-Off. 'I bet a chicken would like runnin' around on a farm.'

'We'll have to see what Mrs Bartley says tomorrow,' said Gran as she snuggled down under her blanket. 'I must say this mattress is very comfortable. I'm sure we'll all get a good night's rest.'

We must have been really tired cos it was late when we woke up. 'Oh, my goodness!' said Gran, looking at her watch. 'Mrs Bartley will be here before long. Come on. Let's have a wash and then we'll go and have breakfast.'

Having a wash every morning hadn't been part of our routine since the tube station bomb. It hadn't seemed important. But Gran insisted we walk over to the toilets where there was soap and water.

'Hands and face!' she said as we parted company outside the lav. 'And don't forget to wash your neck.'

When we came out, Gran inspected All-Off and me – behind our ears and round our necks, even our foreheads.

224

'I'm not going on that train with a couple of dirty lads,' she said. Then she turned to All-Off. 'You will come with us to Yorkshire, won't you? We've got a big old farmhouse with plenty of room. It'll be grand to have children about the place again.'

But All-Off shook his head. 'I'll come to the station to wave you off, missus, but I ain't going with yer. I don't think much of sheep and grass and stuff like that. I'll stay here, thanks. I can manage on my own.'

I wasn't surprised. All-Off had been living by himself for weeks. But I wished he'd come with us. I was going to miss him a lot.

As it turned out, we didn't go to the station the next day. Rose wasn't well enough to travel.

'We need to keep her here for another day,' the doctor told Gran. 'But it won't be long before she's better. Fingers crossed, eh?'

In fact, we waited for two more days, but in all that time, I didn't see either Mum or Rose. Only Gran was allowed to go in at visiting time but she told us they were getting on very nicely. During the day, All-Off and me went back home and took Sheeba for walks while Gran helped the WVS ladies with the cooking.

On the third day, we were in the church hall having a bowl of porridge, when Mrs Bartley arrived. She was looking very pleased with herself, smiling from ear to ear.

'What's happened?' I asked.

'I've got some news,' she said. 'Rose is much better this

morning and the doctor says she can travel to Yorkshire. He'll give you some medicine for her, Mrs Wilson.'

'Oh, that's wonderful,' said Gran. 'I'll make sure I take good care of her.'

'Now I'm going to organise transport to get you to the station,' Mrs Bartley added. Then she paused, looked at me and winked. 'I've got some other news, too.'

'Can we take Sheeba and Feathers on the train?' I asked

She laughed. 'Yes, I'm sure you can. But that's not the news.'

'What is it?'

'I've just talked to the doctor and he said your mother's head wound is well healed. He also said her leg will take time, but she doesn't need to be in hospital. If you can look after her until the cast is taken off, then he'll give permission for her to travel on the train.'

'You mean Mum can come with us to Yorkshire?'

'Yes, that's right.'

Brilliant news! I cheered and laughed so that everybody in the hall turned round to look at me. But I didn't care. Mum was coming with us.

Mrs Bartley went away to find someone to take us to the station and when that was done, she went with Gran to the hospital to fetch Mum and Rose.

'Best if you boys wait here,' said Gran. 'We don't want to bump into that matron again, do we?'

'We'd better get Sheeba and Feathers,' I said to All-Off when Gran had gone. 'We'll be back in no time.'

It didn't take us long to get to Fernlea Road. Once we were

home, all we had to do was find a box to carry Feathers in and clip a lead on Sheeba.

'I'm glad you came with me,' I said to All-Off. 'I couldn't manage the two of them by myself.' Once again, I tried to persuade him to come to Yorkshire, but he just shook his head.

We were walking out of the house when he said, 'What about your dad's banjo?'

How could I forget that? I ran back inside and fetched it from the cupboard under the stairs. I clutched it under my arm, making Dad seem near. Now I'd got everything I needed.

We made it to the Church Hall shortly before Mrs Bartley arrived, pushing Mum in a wheelchair. Gran was pushing Rose who was smiling and looked almost back to normal. We raced over to meet them.

'Billy!' called Rose, holding out her arms. 'Look! I'm better now. And Mum's all right, too, except for her poorly leg.'

Mum looked ever so happy. She was paler and thinner than usual, but that didn't matter. I knew she'd soon be back to her old self with Gran's cooking. She looked very smart, wearing something I'd never seen before – a black and white checked coat with a hat to match.

I gave her a big hug and said, 'You look nice, Mum.'

She smiled. 'Do I really, Billy? The WVS found me the clothes. Mine were ruined.' Then she turned to Mrs Bartley. 'You ladies have been marvellous. I don't know what I'd have done without you.'

Mrs Bartley rested her hand on Mum's shoulder. 'I'm glad to

see that you're recovering well, Mrs Wilson. You'll just have to take care for the next few weeks.'

'Don't you worry,' said Gran. 'I'll make sure she's looked after. My son's got a fine wife and I'm proud of her.' Mum looked really pleased to hear this and she reached up and squeezed Gran's hand.

Not long after, a battered, black van arrived outside the church hall to take us to the station. It was quite old and the engine spluttered so much that I wondered if it would ever get us there.

'It's not a Rolls Royce, I'm afraid,' said Mrs Bartley, 'but it's the best we can do. The WVS kindly lent it to us this morning knowing you wouldn't be able to get to the station without help.'

'Please thank them,' said Mum. 'I'm very grateful.'

We helped Mum out of the wheelchair and, using crutches, she managed to walk to the van. Then the driver gave her a hand to get into the front seat.

'Are you coming, All-Off?' I asked as we lifted Rose into the back.

'Just to the station,' he said. 'I'll see you onto the train and wave you off.'

He climbed into the back of the van followed by Gran and me and we sat on an old carpet on the floor.

'Billy and me have been in a big lorry, Gran,' said Rose, remembering our other trip to the station. She lowered her chin and looked very serious. 'We ran away cos we didn't like it, did we, Billy?'

Gran put her arm round her. 'Well, we won't be running away this time, will we? We're all going to Yorkshire.'

The driver checked we were all safely inside. 'Ready to go?' he said and shut the back doors. Then he started the engine and we set off.

When we arrived at the station, it was crowded. There were a lot of people in uniform – soldiers, sailors, and airmen – most of them carrying huge kit bags and all waiting for trains.

Mrs Bartley hurried over to the ticket office and when she came back she said, 'I got tickets for all of you. You, too, All-Off. You could go up to Yorkshire for a few days.' Then she handed him the ticket. 'You can always return if you want to.'

'Naw. I don't fancy the country, thanks. I expect it'd make me sneeze – all that fresh air. No. I only come here so I could see 'em safe on the train.'

An announcement came over the loud speaker to say that the train for York was arriving shortly and soon it came puffing into the station making a deafening noise, filling the air with white steam. Sheeba started whining and tugged on the lead. I think it was so strange for her that she must have been feeling nervous.

'It's a very big train, ain't it?' Rose said.

'It is,' said Mrs Bartley. 'But you must hurry and find some seats before the train gets too full.'

When the train stopped, the people on the platform surged forward to climb on board. Mrs Bartley waved her hand and called for a porter.

'This lady has a broken leg,' she said, when one came hurrying over. 'Please help her onto the train.'

Instead of helping Mum, he pointed to Sheeba. 'That dog of yours can't get on with you,' he said. 'He'll have to go in the guard's van.' Then he looked at All-Off who was carrying the box with Feathers in it. 'And what have you got there, young man?'

'Nothing,' said All-Off.

'Then why have you got holes in the box, eh? Got a rat in there, have you?'

'She's not a rat, she's a chicken,' said Rose. 'You just leave her alone.'

'Right then,' said the porter, taking hold of Sheeba's lead and tucking Feathers' box under his arm. 'I'll take 'em to the guard's van. They'll be well looked after till you get off the train.'

Rose burst into tears but there was no time to argue. We had to get on board and find a seat.

Another porter came to help Mum and, as she climbed into the train, she turned to Mrs Bartley and said, 'Thank you very much. We shan't forget you. You've been such a help to my family.'

'Yes, thank you,' said Gran. 'You've been grand.'

Once we were on the train, we found that all the compartments seemed to be full. Even the corridor was crammed with people looking for seats so it wasn't easy.

A soldier sitting in one of the compartments saw Mum struggling on her crutches and he stood up, slid open the door and stepped out into the corridor. 'Here, love,' he called. 'You have my seat. You look as though you need one.'

'Thank you,' Mum said, as she struggled inside and sat down.

There were four seats on either side of the compartment. The others were taken by soldiers who looked exhausted as if they hadn't slept for days. Even the luggage racks above them were full to bursting with their kit bags. But as soon as they saw Gran and Rose, two of them got to their feet.

'You and the little girl sit down, missus,' they said. 'We can stand, don't you worry.'

While Gran and Rose took the seats, I stayed out in the corridor. I wasn't ready to say goodbye to All-Off yet. I stood by the open door and called down to him on the platform. 'Come with us, All-Off. It won't be much fun without you.'

But he pretended not to hear and turned away without a word to me or Mrs Bartley. Then he began walking towards the exit waving his hand as if he didn't have a care in the world.

I felt real bad seeing him go like that and I shouted after him, 'You're the best mate I've ever had. Did you know that?' And he stopped in his tracks.

Suddenly I heard banging and, when I leaned out, I saw porters walking along the platform, slamming the doors shut. The guard was standing near the back of the train with his whistle in his mouth, holding a green flag. The train would be leaving any second.

I yelled again, 'I don't want to go to Yorkshire without you!'

Then a porter slammed the door shut, separating me from All-Off. It was too late.

But, as the whistle blew for us to leave, All-Off suddenly spun round. I couldn't believe it! He was running back towards the train which was already moving, puffing slowly down the line. Was it too late for All-Off? He could run like the wind. He was fast. He was racing along the platform, his legs pounding trying to catch up. Recklessly, I grabbed the handle and flung the door wide open.

'Come on, All-Off,' I yelled, 'You can make it.'

Soldiers standing in the corridor were watching him and they called, too.

'Faster!' they shouted. 'Come on! Come on!' And we held out our hands to catch him.

At the very last minute, he flung himself through the open door and we pulled him inside.

'I changed me mind,' he said with a wide grin on his face. And we all fell about laughing.

Once the laughing and the puffing and panting were over, we went into the compartment where Mum was sitting and we settled ourselves on the floor. The train soon left London behind and, as it headed for the green hills of Yorkshire, I thought how lucky I was to have my family and my best mate with me. There was only one person missing – Dad. I clutched his banjo, closed my eyes, and remembered that picnic on Brighton beach. Mum, Dad, Rose and me.

Before the war.

Together.

Acknowledgements

Although I invented the characters in *Billy's Blitz,* the story is based on real events and set in real places. Many people, societies and research departments have given me invaluable help in my attempt to give as accurate a picture as possible of the Blitz in London during 1940.

With thanks to the Wandsworth Heritage Centre, the Imperial War Museum, the London Metropolitan Archives, the London Transport Museum, the Telecommunications Heritage Group and the National Archives. My thanks also to David Cromarty for his expert knowledge of trains and to my wonderful editors, Charlie Sheppard and Chloe Sackur, for their guidance and support.

Run Rabbit Run

BARBARA MITCHELHILL

When Lizzie's dad refuses to fight in the Second World War, the police come looking to arrest him. Desperate to stay together, Lizzie and her brother Freddie go on the run with him, hiding from the police in idyllic Whiteway. But when their past catches up with them, they're forced to leave and it becomes more and more difficult to stay together as a family. Will they be able to? And will they ever find a place, like Whiteway, where they will be safe again?

Nominated for the Carnegie Medal

'A well-told story showing that bravery comes in many guises.'
Carousel

9781849392495 £6.99